YELLOWSTONE NATIONAL PARK

Eye of the Grizzly

Adventures with the Parkers

Mike Graf

Illustrated by
Marjorie Leggitt

FALCONGUIDES

GUILFORD, CONNECTICUT
HELENA, MONTANA

AN IMPRINT OF GLOBE PEQUOT PRESS

FALCONGUIDES®

Text © 2007, 2012 Mike Graf
Illustrations © 2007, 2012 Marjorie Leggitt

FalconGuides is an imprint of Globe Pequot Press.
Falcon, FalconGuides, and Outfit Your Mind are registered trademarks of Morris Book Publishing, LLC.

Photo credits:
Licensed by Shutterstock.com: Title page; 3: © Alfie Photography (bottom); 4: © creativex; 6; 8: © East Village Images; 10; 11; 13: © Tom Reichner; 14–15; 16; 18; 19; 24: © Jeff Banke; 25: © Julie Lubick; 27; 29: © Julie Lubick; 31 (top left); 33: © Tim Walden; 34; 38–39; 40; 45; 48: © Kenneth Keifer; 51; 52–53: © Ffooter, 58; 59; 65: © dmyphotos; 68: © Catherine Lall, 71: © Audrey Snider-Bell; 73: © Olga Lipatova, 76: © Olena Pivnenko; 79; 91; 92: © Kane513; 94–95
© Mike Graf: 15; 30; 31 (bottom left, top and bottom right); 38 (inset); 42–43; 54; 55; 56; 63; 74; 75; 86
Map courtesy of National Park Service

Illustrations: Marjorie Leggitt
Models for twins: Amanda and Ben Frazier

Project editor: David Legere

Library of Congress Cataloging-in-Publication Data is available on file.

ISBN 978-0-7627-7972-7

Printed in the United States of America

"How much spray is in there?" James asked.

"About four seconds' worth," the clerk replied.

James's mom, Kristen, looked at the bear-spray canister with apprehension. "Is there anything else we should know about it?"

"Yes," the clerk continued, "use this only as a last line of defense. Also, make sure the wind doesn't blow the spray in any other direction except at the bear. You don't want this to get in your eyes. And, it is most effective the first time it's used. If you have to spray a bear, get out of the area afterward, as fast as possible."

"Have you ever needed it?" James's dad, Robert, asked.

"Not yet," the clerk answered. "But I often hike alone, so I always carry spray with me, especially when I'm anywhere near Yellowstone. There are four of you. The larger the group, the safer you are."

Mom, Dad, James, and his twin sister, Morgan, were in the town of West Yellowstone. This was their last stop before entering Yellowstone National Park. They were at a sporting goods store purchasing supplies. Dad was also looking at fly-fishing gear.

"Should we get one or two of those cans of bear spray?" Dad asked.

"Two," Mom responded. "It's better to be safe than sorry."

"I need to get a fishing permit too," Dad said to the clerk.

Dad filled out the permit and paid. They loaded their gear into the car and drove through town, heading for the park entrance station.

Mom rolled down the window and showed the ranger the family's annual national park pass. They entered Yellowstone National Park.

Dad stared at the scenery in awe. "This is what I love about national parks," he said. "They are wild, beautiful, unspoiled places."

The west entrance road followed the Madison River as it meandered along. The hills nearby were full of pine trees. Many of the trees looked like poles without anything growing on them.

"What happened to the forest?" James asked.

"There was a huge fire here years ago," Mom answered.

The family gazed out the windows at the scenery and looked for animals.

"In Yellowstone," Dad explained, "some kind of animal is liable to be out there somewhere."

"I hope we see a bear," Morgan said.

"What kind?" James asked.

"A grizzly," Morgan replied, "from a safe distance."

"I want to see a wolf," Mom said. "They've been reintroduced to the park, and there are many packs living here now."

"I want to see a moose!" James exclaimed. "What about you, Dad? What animal do you want to see the most?"

"Me? Definitely a bison."

In 1988, unusually dry conditions caused a series of fires started by lightning to burn out of control. In the end, about 36 percent of Yellowstone burned. Twenty-five thousand firefighters were involved in fighting the blazes and $120 million was spent. About 300 large mammals died in the fires. The first snows of September finally helped extinguish the blazes.

Some changes have occurred because of the fires, including:

- New lodgepole pines are growing throughout the park. These trees benefited from the fire. It helped open their cones, and ash from the fire fertilized the soil they grow in.
- Aspens are growing where they had not previously existed.
- Yellowstone's moose thrived in old-growth forests. Because a great deal of those forests burned, there are now fewer moose in the park.

"Look at all those cars stopped ahead," Mom pointed out.
Mom slowed down as she approached the line of cars.

"It must be a pretty bad accident," Morgan commented.

Mom inched closer to the car in front of them. She put on the brakes and stopped. Several cars behind her did the same thing. "We're jammed in good now," she said.

The Parkers noticed people piling out of their cars with cameras.

James gazed toward a meadow. "It isn't an accident. Look!"

A bunch of large brown animals were way out in the meadow. Some of the animals were walking near the river. Others were chewing on grass.

"It's a herd of elk!" Dad announced.

"There are more over here, right next to the road!" James called out.

"Here, let me park the car," Mom said. She drove into a pull-out. Everyone piled out of the car. James grabbed the binoculars. Morgan took her camera.

The family walked quietly through the trees for a better view.

"There are elk all over the place!" Morgan exclaimed.

"And they're huge!" James added.

"Don't get too close," Mom warned.

James pointed to the people scattered about the meadow. "What about them?"

"I think," Dad said, "that those people shouldn't be where they are."

Morgan, James, Mom, and Dad stayed put.

"Elk look like miniature horses," James said.

Morgan started counting. "I'll bet there's at least fifty out there," she estimated.

"And all females," Mom said. "None of them have antlers."

In Yellowstone, visitors should respect all wildlife and consider all animals potentially dangerous. General wildlife viewing rules include:

- Do not approach wildlife.
- Do not feed, disturb, or harass wildlife.
- All visitors must stay at least twenty-five yards away from all wildlife except for bears; at least 100 yards must be kept between visitors and bears at all times.
- Bison are particularly dangerous. Although they may appear slow and docile, they can run up to thirty miles per hour, over three times as fast as any person. Bison have charged and severely gored visitors in Yellowstone.

"Hey, James," Morgan suggested, "let's keep track of what animals we see and where on the park map. Okay?"

"Good idea," James replied.

"Let's head back to the car now," Mom suggested. "I have a feeling that we'll see quite a few more animals before our week here is up."

James and Morgan climbed in the backseat and immediately unfolded their Yellowstone map.

James wrote "At least 50 elk" on the map on a spot about five miles west of Madison. "Our first animal sighting," he said.

Mom maneuvered the car onto the road. In a moment, they were back on the highway, heading toward Madison Junction.

Dad turned around and beamed at the twins. "Old Faithful, here we come!"

Mom drove into a giant parking lot filled with cars.

The family clambered out of their car. They looked at all the RVs, trucks, cars, and motorcycles. "People from all over the United States are here," James said. "There's a Florida license plate. And one from New York."

"That's quite a long drive!" Dad said.

"I'll bet Old Faithful's up that way," Morgan pointed. "Look at all the people."

The family walked toward a wooden walkway.

Morgan, James, Mom, and Dad found a group of seats on benches that partially surrounded the geyser.

Meanwhile, a safe distance away, Old Faithful's cone bubbled, splashed, and spurted out water, accompanied by small puffs of steam.

"I wonder when it's going to erupt," James said.

"Supposedly close to 6:02 p.m.," a person next to James said.

"Thanks," James said. "What time is it, Dad?"

"It's 5:45," Dad responded. "So not too much longer."

Suddenly, the steam coming from Old Faithful puffed out more intensely. Hot water splashed over the top of the cone. Morgan and James leaned forward.

But then the steam and water from Old Faithful subsided.

"A false alarm, I guess," Mom concluded.

"I can wait a few more minutes," James said.

Dad looked at his family and grinned.

WHAT A BLAST!

The Washburn expedition of 1870 named Old Faithful because of its regular eruptions. Old Faithful erupts every 40 to 107 minutes. Its average eruption is four minutes long, and it pumps out between 4,000 and 8,400 gallons of water each time it goes off.

To predict Old Faithful's next eruption, use a clock with a second hand to time a current eruption until it completely stops. If the total time is less than four minutes, the next eruption will be in 40 to 60 minutes. If the eruption is longer than four minutes, the next eruption will be in 75 to 100+ minutes. Predicted eruption times are posted at the Old Faithful Visitor Center.

"What's so funny?" Morgan asked.

"Look around," Dad replied. "Doesn't it seem like we're at a ball game?"

Morgan scanned the crowd on the benches. "It does!"

"Get your popcorn, peanuts, and hot dogs," Dad announced in a vendorlike voice.

James laughed. "Cotton candy, soda, pretzels."

"Geyser burgers, geyser souvenirs, geyser snow cones, right here," Morgan said.

Mom smiled. She took on the voice of a television commentator and whispered into a pretend microphone. "Here we are, ladies and gentlemen. We're at Old Faithful, waiting for the world's most famous geyser to erupt."

The crowd hushed. The Parkers stopped playing and looked at Old Faithful. Small spurts of water continued to percolate out of the cone with a gentle, consistent vent of steam. But it wasn't erupting.

"Over there!" Morgan called out.

A large animal was slowly trudging across the geyser basin.

"A bison!" Dad exclaimed.

The bison meandered between Old Faithful and the boardwalk.

"It shouldn't be out there," Mom said.

James joked, "I guess it didn't read the sign."

Morgan started snapping pictures of the bison.

The bison took another step. Its hind leg broke through the soil and collapsed into the ground.

The bison pulled its foot out of the hole and shook it around.

"I think it just got scalded," Mom announced.

The startled bison ran around erratically. Then it shifted directions and hastily stomped toward Morgan, James, Mom, and Dad.

"Look out!" Dad shouted.

Mom grabbed James and pulled him out of his seat. Dad took Morgan's arm. The family and the spectators nearby quickly abandoned the benches.

The bison leaped off the fragile soil and onto the boardwalk. It trotted toward the parking lot.

The bison slowed its pace and calmly plodded along again. The Parkers returned to their seats.

"I wonder if it was burned badly," Morgan said.

Suddenly, the large crowd started counting down: "17, 16, 15, 14, 13, 12, 11 . . ."

Morgan, James, Mom, and Dad watched Old Faithful. The geyser continued to send up wisps of steam, but it didn't appear any more active.

Yellowstone's thermal areas are beautiful, but they are also dangerous. The water in these features is often at or above the boiling point. The soil nearby is thin, breaks easily, and often covers scalding water. Be safe around thermal areas:

- Stay on boardwalks and marked trails.
- Closely supervise young children.
- Keep pets out of thermal areas.

The crowd continued counting: "10, 9, 8, 7, 6, 5 . . ."

Morgan got her camera ready.

"Here goes," Dad called out.

"4, 3, 2, 1." The crowd finished the countdown. But Old Faithful didn't erupt.

James looked at Dad's watch. "It's 6:02," he informed his family.

"I guess Old Faithful isn't that faithful," Morgan stated.

James turned around to see the bison walking slowly away in the meadows beyond the parking lot.

At 6:05, Morgan decided to pull out her journal.

Dear Diary,

Guess what? We're sitting with hundreds of people waiting for the world's most famous geyser, Old Faithful, to erupt. I can't wait to see it.

But Old Faithful is only one of many geysers in the park. James and I have already looked at the map. What other geysers do we want to see? Grotto, Castle, Beehive, Steamboat, and Lone Star, to name a few. Then there are all of Yellowstone's hot pools, mud pots, and steam vents. There's so much to see here.

Speaking of seeing things, we've already seen a huge herd of elk and a wandering bison.

A towering plume of water blasted out of Old Faithful's cone.

"There it goes!" Dad exclaimed.

Morgan put her pen down.

The water shot up over 100 feet high. Drifts of warm mist from the spray spread across the air and showered the soil nearby.

"It looks like they put a giant fire hydrant in there," James said.

Old Faithful continued to shoot out water and steam. Morgan snapped pictures. The powerful spray lasted several minutes, then gradually subsided. Soon the height of the water was forty feet. Then thirty feet. The last few moments of Old Faithful's eruption appeared to be mostly steam.

Everyone clapped after Old Faithful's performance.

"I want to see more geysers!" James exclaimed.

"I imagine we will," Dad said.

After watching Old Faithful, the family took a short walk around nearby Geyser Hill. They passed many uniquely shaped geysers, pools, and steam vents.

A person was sitting on the wooden boardwalk near Doublet Pool writing down notes.

Morgan, James, Mom, and Dad stood by and looked. Two adjoining pools of hot water glistened sapphire blue and were surrounded by a whitish edge. The water in the picturesque pool bubbled and steamed.

The person writing looked up at the Parkers. "Hello."

"Hi," Morgan replied.

"Can I ask what you're writing?" Dad asked.

"Sure," the man replied. "I'm a geyser gazer. That means it's my hobby to record the behavior of Yellowstone's thermal features, which includes some of the changes they go through."

"Does this pool change?" Morgan asked.

"Doublet Pool is one of my favorites," the man replied. "It goes through a little cycle of rising, bubbling, vibrating, and thumping. All of it happens very subtly. You have to hang out and see."

"It's very beautiful," Morgan commented.

"Are there any others you'd recommend?" Dad inquired.

The man smiled. "Everyone has his or her personal favorite. But take your time and try to see some away from the crowds. Perhaps you'll end up being a geyser gazer, like me." The man put down his journal. "I'm Tom," he introduced himself.

"Hi, Tom," James said, then introduced himself, Morgan, and his parents.

The family watched Doublet Pool for a moment longer. "You've given us some good advice," Mom said. "Thanks."

James crawled out of the family's tent and sat on the picnic table bench nearby. He gazed through the binoculars at the meadow beyond the campground. So far, though, James saw nothing moving.

James opened up his journal and wrote.

This is James Parker reporting.

It's an icy morning in Yellowstone. There's frost on the windshield of the car, and I even have my gloves on. But I guess that's what it's like when you're camped in the Rocky Mountains at 8,000 feet. It doesn't matter that it's the middle of summer.

My parents are letting me plan out what to see in the park. It's quite a responsibility! But I'm following the park map and our guidebook for suggestions. The main park road is like a figure-eight loop. We entered the park from the west near Madison and are leaving toward the south near Lewis Lake. Hopefully, we'll get to see many of the sights in between.

I feel like we are on a wilderness safari trek. I'm up early this morning, keeping an eye out for wildlife. Which I think I just spotted . . .

I'll report more soon.

From Yellowstone,

James Parker

James picked up his binoculars and scanned the horizon.

On the far side of the meadow, a brown dot had emerged from the trees. James focused the binoculars on the animal. "Hmm," he muttered.

"What's up?" Mom asked from inside the tent.

"Sorry. I was trying to be quiet," James responded. "But I think there's a bull elk off in the distance. I can see its antlers."

"Really?" Dad asked. "How far away?"

"On the far side of the meadow," James answered.

"I want to see it!" Morgan called out.

In a minute, Morgan was bundled up, sitting next to James. James handed Morgan the binoculars.

Morgan spotted the elk then began searching the rest of the area. "That's not the only one." She pointed to another part of the meadow. "See?" She handed James the binoculars.

James saw a herd of female elk, also called cow elk, scattered about. "I can't believe I missed them," James said.

The elk took off running. They bounded through the grass and in an instant were in the forest.

"I wonder why they all ran away," Morgan said.

After breakfast, Morgan, James, Mom, and Dad got ready for sightseeing. James highlighted areas on the map near where they were camped. He showed his family all the places he had circled.

"That ought to keep us busy," Mom commented.

"And if we have time at the end of the day," Dad said, "I have a surprise place to take us."

"A surprise?" James asked.

"You'll see," Dad answered.

Dad parked the car at Biscuit Basin. The Parkers piled out of the car and headed onto the boardwalk. They approached Sapphire Pool. A cloud of steam blew up into the air and drifted onto the family. An instant later, the steam cleared.

They gazed into a large, deep pool.

"It looks like a giant swimming pool," James said.

"It's way too hot to swim in there," Dad reminded him.

Morgan took a picture. "I wonder how deep it is."

Shell Spring, Biscuit Basin

James noticed a small spray of water in the distance. "Hey, there's a little geyser out there!"

The family watched the small geyser.

James looked at his map. "I think that might be Jewel Geyser."

They walked along the path and passed by Shell Spring and bubbling Avoca Spring.

"These thermal things are everywhere!" Dad exclaimed.

Morgan, James, Mom, and Dad reached the end of the boardwalk. A dirt trail led toward Mystic Falls. On a nearby tree, a posted sign read:

WARNING: BEAR FREQUENTING AREA.
THERE IS NO GUARANTEE OF YOUR SAFETY ON THIS TRAIL.

"Well, that's a bit unnerving," Mom commented.

James looked back toward Biscuit Basin. "It seems like everyone's over there and there's hardly anyone out here."

"Yes, we are entering the Yellowstone wilderness for the first time," Dad stated. "I guess it's time to get ready."

Dad took off his pack and laid it on the ground. He pulled out the two bear-spray canisters and handed one to Mom.

Mom and Dad each clipped the canisters onto their belts. Dad slipped his pack back over his shoulders, and the family headed out on the Mystic Falls Trail.

They quickly entered a small canyon with a gurgling stream running through it.

"We should make noise to alert the bears," Dad said. "Hey, bear!" he shouted.

James copied Dad. "Hey, bear!"

The canyon narrowed. Soon they approached an area with sculpted rock formations. Just beyond was Mystic Falls.

Morgan, James, Mom, and Dad stared at the 100-foot-tall waterfall. "There's steam coming out of the top," Morgan realized.

"Not just there," James said. "All over it."

Mom looked at the unusual waterfall. "Maybe that's why they call it 'Mystic.'"

They walked to the bottom of the falls. A trickle of water seeped from some rocks alongside the trail into a tiny pool next to the stream.

James reached down and put his finger in the water. "Ow!" he exclaimed. "It's hot!"

Morgan put her finger in the large stream below the falls. "It's cold over here."

"We should be careful where we put our hands, then," Dad said.

The family sat down on some rocks.

Dad took off his pack and opened it. He pulled out some trail mix and passed it around. Morgan took a small handful of the snack and put it in her mouth. Then she stood up and walked around, hoping to get different angles for pictures.

After snacking, they climbed the switchbacks above the falls.

"Hey, bear!" Dad shouted.

BEAR COUNTRY
Store all food in vehicle
Read bulletin board regulations
All wildlife are dangerous

"Hey, bear!" Morgan echoed.

Soon they came to an overlook.

"There's the Old Faithful area," Mom pointed out. "And all the places nearby we've been seeing today."

After spending time at the viewpoint, the family hiked down the trail and back to their car.

Next, they hiked to Fairy Falls and ate a picnic lunch at its base. Many other people also stopped there, took pictures, and sat by the small pool of water underneath the falls.

On the way back, Mom noticed a faint path up a small hill. "I wonder what's up there."

Mom led her family up the trail. Once at the top, they got a bird's-eye view of massive Grand Prismatic Spring.

"That pool is huge!" Morgan exclaimed.

"How did you know to come up here?" Dad inquired.

Mom shrugged her shoulders. "I don't know, just a hunch."

The family continued sightseeing. They visited the Fountain Paint Pot Trail and Firehole Lake Drive. James kept track of the sites they went to on the map.

"It's endless, the things we could see here," Mom commented.

"But now," Dad stated enthusiastically, "our little secret adventure."

Morgan and James looked at Dad.

They drove toward Madison Junction. Near the junction, Dad turned onto Firehole Canyon Drive. They entered a scenic canyon with a small river running through it.

"It's pretty remote in here," Morgan commented.

Dad smiled. "Exactly."

The car climbed a narrow, winding road. They came to a parking area.

"Get on your swimsuits and grab your towels," Dad announced. "We're going in!"

After quickly changing, the Parkers piled out of the car. At the top of some wooden stairs, they looked down at the Firehole River. Dozens of people were wading, walking, and swimming in it.

"This is one place where they allow swimming in Yellowstone," Dad explained. "So it's not totally a secret."

Morgan, James, Mom, and Dad headed down the stairs and put their towels down near some rocks.

James took a step into the water. "It's warm. Like a pool."

Dad explained, "This water is heated by the thermal areas we just came from. By the time the water gets here, it's the perfect temperature for swimming."

"How did you know about this?" James asked.

"The guide-book!" Dad replied.

For the rest of the afternoon, the family swam and rested alongside the Firehole River.

Grand Prismatic

"That video we had to watch at the permit office was interesting," Morgan commented.

"I'll say," Dad replied. "And even though *this* trail was an easy three miles, now we know how to backpack in bear country."

James tied the end of a rope to a large rock. "That's why I'm doing this."

James slung the rock up toward a pole fastened between two trees. The rock slammed against the pole and fell back down to the ground.

James smiled. "I'll get it next time." He picked up the rock and threw it higher. This time the rock sailed over the pole and came down on the other side with the rope still attached.

James tugged on the rope and began to lift his backpack off the ground. Morgan came over and helped by pushing the backpack up until it was out of her reach. Then Morgan helped James pull on the rope. Soon James's pack was with the others', snug against the bear pole, twenty feet off the ground.

"That ought to keep the bears out," Dad commented.

They walked over to Grebe Lake.

The lake was surrounded by forested hills. The family found a place to sit down near the rocky shoreline to enjoy the sunset.

Mom fixed the binoculars on a large bird as it drifted in circles above the lake. The bird suddenly plunged toward the water and disappeared beneath the surface. An instant later, it came up with a small fish in its talons and flew away.

"Ospreys sure know how to fish," Mom said.

Morgan pointed to another bird soaring overhead. "Is that an osprey too?"

Mom looked up with the binoculars. "It's hard to focus because it's moving so much." Mom watched the bird a moment longer. "I think it's a bald eagle!"

"How do you know?" Dad asked.

"It's larger than the osprey, and I can see its white head and tail."

Mom passed the binoculars around. The family continued watching the birds and the sunset. Big billowing clouds had formed in the evening sky.

Three hundred twenty types of birds have been spotted in Yellowstone, and 148 of them nest in the park. Some of the birds seen in the park include the **whooping crane, bald eagle, peregrine falcon, brown pelican, trumpeter swan, osprey, loon, harlequin duck,** and **great horned owl.**

Adult bald eagles are completely white on their heads and tails. Immature bald eagles may not be totally white and are often mistaken for golden eagles, which also live in the park.

Ospreys are slightly smaller than bald eagles. They have white bellies and white heads with a dark streak through their eyes. Their wings are narrow with dark patches, and they have a bend at the wrist of their wings.

"I wonder what other animals are out here," James said.

"We did see an awful lot of poop along the trail," Dad added.

"Scat," Mom corrected.

Dad smiled. James and Morgan laughed.

James picked up a smooth rock. He aimed low and skipped it across the water.

"Three!" Morgan counted for him.

Morgan flung a rock and James counted. "Six!" he announced.

Morgan and James skipped several more rocks before the family climbed the hill to their campsite.

Once there, Morgan turned on a lantern inside their tent. They each started getting ready for bed.

Sometime during the night, Morgan woke up. There was an eerie whistling sound outside. She sat up and listened. "Do you hear that?"

"Yes," James whispered. "What do you think it is?"

The whistling sound continued.

"It kind of sounds like howling," Morgan said.

Mom raised her head. "I think it's the wind blowing through the trees."

"It sounds spooky," James said. "Like there are ghosts out there."

Suddenly, light flickered outside. For a brief second, the family's shadows were silhouetted on the walls of the tent. A few seconds later, there was a distant rumble of thunder.

The wind picked up and lightning flickered again. Thunder boomed more loudly. A few raindrops began to pelt down.

Morgan scrunched closer to Mom. "That one sounded like it was close to our tent."

The family listened to the storm. The tent rattled in the wind and the rain fly rustled continuously.

At some point, they fell asleep.

. . .

The morning weather was calm. James elbowed his father. "Come on. You wanted me to wake you up early to go fishing."

Dad yawned and blinked his eyes. "Is that what I said?"

Morgan, James, and Dad put on warm clothes and trudged down to the bear pole. Dad lowered their packs and got out the fishing gear. He hoisted the packs back up. They took the three fishing rods to the shore of Grebe Lake.

"This spot looks as good as any," Dad announced.

Dad set up his fishing rod. He tied on one of the flies he had purchased in West Yellowstone then pulled out ten feet of line.

"Watch this." Dad whipped the line back and forth in the air. "See the backward motion I'm making that creates an *S* in my line? That's when you cast forward."

Dad cast his line. As it lowered to the lake, the fly gently dropped onto the surface of the water. Dad let it drift for a few seconds and then slowly eased in the line a few inches at a time. "That's the technique," he said. "Let the bait act like a real fly landing on the water."

Dad helped the twins set up. Eventually, they were spread out, fishing. Each time they cast, they slowly pulled in the fly, just as Dad had explained.

Two birds with oval-shaped heads and long, pointy beaks swam together near the lakeshore. "I think," Dad called over to James and Morgan, "that those birds gave this lake its name."

"Those are grebes?" James inquired.

"I think so, but Mom would know for sure."

James heard some footsteps crunching behind him. He quickly turned around. A man in a ranger uniform walked up.

"Good morning," the ranger said.

"Hi," James answered.

Dad put down his rod and signaled for Morgan to do the same. Dad and Morgan walked over to join James and the ranger.

"How's the fishing this morning?" the ranger asked.

"So far we haven't caught a thing," James answered.

"Just remember, it's catch-and-release only here. Unless you snare a nonnative trout," the ranger said.

"Got it," Dad replied.

"By the way, do you have a backcountry permit?" the ranger asked.

"It's attached to the outside of our tent," James answered. "We're camped right up the hill from those bear poles."

"You're in 4G3," the ranger stated. "It's a fantastic site. Lucky you."

HEALTH FOOD

> Yellowstone's trout are very important to the animals that live in the park. Bald eagles, ospreys, otters, pelicans, and bears all eat fish. Since no waters in Yellowstone are stocked, adult fish are necessary to keep populations healthy. Therefore, native fish such as the cutthroat trout, grayling, and mountain whitefish are catch-and-release only.

"By the way, the far end of the lake near the lily pads seems to be the hot spot lately," the ranger suggested. "You might try over there."

"Thanks," Dad replied. "The fish weren't biting here anyway."

Morgan, James, and Dad walked back to the trail. Mom was climbing down the hill with her art supplies.

"Good morning!" Mom said cheerfully. She kissed Robert and hugged her children. "I'm going to sketch the lake while the water is calm."

"Sounds great," Dad commented. "We're going to try fishing in another spot for a little while."

Dad and the twins tromped toward the place the ranger had suggested. They soon spotted a part of the lake full of lily pads.

"I guess this is where the ranger meant," Dad said.

They left the trail and walked toward the lake. Morgan stopped. "Wait!" she warned.

A large moose was wading near the shore. It dipped its head below the lily pads and came up with a mouthful of wet grass. The moose slowly chewed on the grass while water dripped out of the sides of its mouth.

"It's too bad Mom isn't seeing this," Dad stated.

"Do you want to fish here now?" James asked.

"Not really," Dad said. "I don't want to bother the moose, they can be quite aggressive and dangerous. We should keep our distance."

Dad looked at his watch. "It's 8:30 already. We'll have to fish again somewhere else on the trip."

After breakfast, they packed up and hiked back to their car at the

trailhead. When they arrived, Morgan opened up the trail registry. She read the notes about animals that other hikers had spotted. "Wolves, bison, black bear, and deer," Morgan said. Then she signed the registry and wrote, "Bald eagle, osprey, and moose."

"We saw animals no one else did," Mom stated. "That's great!"

Dad drove toward the Mammoth area while James caught up with his map.

Dad slowed the car down behind a line of cars.

Morgan leaned forward. "I wonder what it is this time."

Three animals trotted across a distant hillside. Smaller than deer, they had white and brown patches on their bodies and little pointed antlers on their heads.

"Pronghorn!" Mom called out.

Dad pulled over and stopped the car. They watched the pronghorn until the animals bounded over the hill and out of sight.

"Let's walk up there to see if there are any more," Mom suggested.

While climbing, James saw a curved white animal bone in a small nearby ravine. "Whoa!" he called out. "Follow me."

At the bottom of the ravine, James walked up to the skull of a bighorn. He bent down to grab the horns.

Mom stopped James. "No. Wait. In national parks, we're supposed to leave everything just as we found it."

"Take only pictures and leave only footprints," Morgan reminded her brother.

James backed up a bit. "How long do you think it's been dead?"

A gust of wind picked up. It gathered strength and blew James's ball cap right off his head.

The ball cap tumbled along past the bighorn skull and up the other side of the hill. It kept rolling until it finally got stuck on a small bush. The cap shook as if the next big breeze would blow it away again.

"I'll get it," James announced. He scrambled after the hat, but it broke free and rolled farther away.

Finally, James caught up to the cap, grabbed it, and put it back on his head. Then he stood up and took a quick breath.

Just across a clearing, James saw a black bear clawing at a fallen tree. It put its front feet on the log and tried to roll it over. After several tries, the tree finally shifted and the bear dug underneath it. *I don't even think it knows I'm here,* James thought.

Mom saw the bear too. "Come on, let's head up to James and watch!"

Morgan, Mom, and Dad joined James.

Dad checked his bear-spray canister.

"It's not a grizzly, is it?" Morgan asked.

"I don't think so," Mom said. "It has pointed ears, and it doesn't have a hump between its shoulders."

A CLOSER LOOK

It is not always easy to tell the difference between a grizzly and a black bear. But there are some things that can help. Grizzlies are generally larger (if they are adults). They have dish-shaped faces, shorter and more-rounded ears, and a distinct hump between their shoulders. Black bears have a straight face profile, more-pointed ears, and don't have a shoulder hump. Grizzlies are often lighter in color, but not always. Black bears can be black, brown, or cinnamon colored, so color can be misleading.

"That doesn't mean it isn't dangerous," Dad warned.

"But it *is* at least 100 yards away," Mom estimated.

Morgan, James, Mom, and Dad slowly backed up. The bear left the log and meandered away from them, across a plateau. It turned and glanced back at the family. Then it stood up on its hind legs and sniffed the air.

The Parkers stayed close together while backing away from the bear.

The bear stared at the family for a minute, then lumbered away.

"That was pretty cool," James commented.

"And the bear was far away," Dad observed. "But I have to admit, I was a bit nervous."

They finished driving to Mammoth Hot Springs. Dad parked the car and everyone piled out.

Morgan, James, Mom, and Dad walked along the boardwalk that skirted the Mammoth terraces.

They came to Palette Spring. This unusual thermal feature was full of colored, steaming terraces and flowing water.

"It looks so soft and cushiony," Morgan described.

"I think it looks like a Roman bath for gods and goddesses," Mom said.

"I think it looks like overflowing soapsuds filled with melted hot chocolate with marshmallows on top!" James blurted out.

"You're getting hungry, aren't you?" Morgan asked James.

James nodded.

Morgan took several pictures of Palette Spring. The family left the terraces and walked by Liberty Cap, a large, dry, solitary cone near the base of the hot springs.

"That sure is a bizarre formation," Dad said.

They crossed the lawn in front of the Mammoth visitor center and walked toward the parking lot.

James noticed all the people with cameras standing around. "I wonder what's going on."

As Morgan, James, Mom, and Dad approached their car, they saw a herd of elk lying down on the lawn.

A ranger was standing between the visitors and the elk.

"He's trying to keep people away," James realized.

Morgan started taking pictures. "I can't believe we're seeing these animals so close up!"

"There are sixteen of them," James announced.

They walked around the crowd and back to their car.

"It's been quite a day," Dad stated. He pulled out of the Mammoth parking lot and they drove to Indian Creek campground for the night.

After breakfast, the family packed up camp and headed south toward Norris Geyser Basin and Artist Paint Pots. Along the way, they passed a giant, steaming hillside by the side of the road.

James looked at his map. "That must be Roaring Mountain."

"It looks like a large factory," Mom said.

"Just another of Yellowstone's amazing thermal features," Dad said. "There are more of them here than in the rest of the world combined."

Morgan rolled down her window and tried to take a picture.

James stared at the steaming hill. "I wonder what the early explorers thought when they saw that."

"Probably the same thing we're thinking," Mom said. "'What in the world is causing something like that?'"

Dad drove past Norris Junction. A few miles later, he took the turnoff for the Artist Paint Pots trailhead and parked the car. James grabbed his journal as he got out.

"What's that for?" Morgan asked.

"You'll see," James replied.

After hiking a short distance, Morgan, James, Mom, and Dad came to a wooden walkway. There were areas of boiling, hissing, and steaming water nearby.

"Being in Yellowstone is like being on a nature television show," Morgan said.

The Parkers followed the trail up a hill. They approached a circular wooden fence surrounding what looked like a large hole in the ground.

A weird sound came from inside the fence.

James got there first. He stopped and looked into a pit of plopping mud.

Dad joined James and stared into the pit.

The Parkers watched one splat of mud after another shoot up into the air and plop onto the ground.

"Mud pots are amazing!" Dad commented.

James took out his journal and wrote.

Geyser Gazer Feature #1

The Artist Paint Pots Mud Pit

I'm standing here looking at the Artist Paint Pots mud pot. The mud is making a "bloop, bloop, bloop" sound every few seconds. The mud is thick and gooey and looks like gray paint. I guess that's why it's called "Artist Paint Pots." The mud is shooting up about ten feet in the air and splattering all around the hole. This whole thing is about the size of a small swimming pool.

I want to jot down notes about some of these thermal features. That way, when I come back years from now, I can check my notes and see if they've changed!

Reporting from Yellowstone,

James Parker

"It's neat that you are recording this," Dad said.

James looked at his father and smiled.

Mom drove the family over to Norris Geyser Basin. "Let's do a little more sight-seeing while we're in the neighborhood," she suggested.

The molten hot rock beneath Yellowstone is as close as one and a half to three miles below the ground. That's because the Earth's crust beneath Yellowstone is so thin. The worldwide average is more than forty-five miles. Water in Yellowstone seeps below the Earth's surface and gets heated there. As the heated water moves back toward the surface, it passes through minerals, cracks, and various soil conditions. This is what causes the variety of thermal features at Yellowstone:

- **Mud Pots:** These are acidic hot springs that contain very little water. The mud in mud pots is caused by organisms in the Earth changing gas into an acid, which breaks down rocks into clay. Then, wet, gaseous mud often bubbles up as a mud pot.

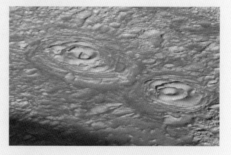

- **Hot Springs:** These hot pools of water can be seen throughout Yellowstone's thermal areas. Colors in these pools are created by light infraction, organisms in the water, and minerals. Grand Prismatic Spring is 250 by 380 feet, about the size of a professional base-ball field. This makes it the largest hot spring in the park and one of the world's largest.

- **Geysers:** These are hot springs with constricted plumbing. The tight cracks that the water travels through underground cause pressure to build up. Once the pressure is too much to contain, the eruption starts. Yellowstone has more than 300 geysers, with Old Faithful being the most famous (but not the largest or the most predictable).

- **Fumaroles:** Water vapor and other gases escape from holes in the ground, creating steam vents called fumaroles. Sometimes the steam is so forceful that the ground nearby trembles. Fumaroles also can make loud hissing or roaring sounds.

The family passed an information station. A sign labeled Norris as "the most active thermal area in the park" and "a steaming landscape of small geysers and colorful hot water features."

The Parkers walked along a wooden path. They soon came to Steamboat Geyser. They gazed at the area of devastation surrounding it.

James read the sign. "This is the world's tallest geyser!" he said.

"Should we wait for it to erupt?" Morgan asked.

Dad also read the sign. "Apparently, that could be a long time."

Steamboat Geyser can be dormant and not erupt for decades, making eruptions difficult to predict. Usually before an eruption, Steamboat has periods of increased splashing in the cone. Sometimes these turn out to be only a minor eruption of ten to sixty feet. But, if you are lucky, you might see Steamboat shoot out water over 380 feet into the air, making it the world's tallest geyser!

"Promise us we'll try and see at least one more geyser erupt before we go," James pleaded.

"Promise," Dad replied.

The family finished hiking through the Norris area. They passed other named thermal features such as Echinus Geyser, Green Dragon Spring, Porkchop Geyser, Pearl Geyser, Vixen Geyser, and Minute Geyser.

"You've gotta love these names!" Dad said.

Eventually, they approached Constant Geyser.

The small geyser shot up a spray of water ten feet into the air.

"There it goes!" James called out.

"I guess it lived up to its name," Dad said.

Morgan smiled. "There's your 'one more' geyser!"

"I meant one more *big* geyser!" James explained.

The family trudged back to the car.

"Okay," James announced. "Here we go."

The Parkers were at the beginning of Uncle Tom's Trail.

After walking down some concrete steps, they came to the first of a series of steep metal stairways fixed into the side of the cliff. They stepped carefully onto the stairs.

CLIFF HANGER

Uncle Tom's Trail at the Grand Canyon of the Yellowstone might be the most unusual trail in the park.

"Uncle" Tom Richardson built the trail between 1898 and 1903. He led visitors down it and included a bridge crossing and picnic as part of his original tour. The trail used to include 528 steps and rope ladders. Now there are 328 steps down to the viewing area near the bottom of the canyon. But it can be quite strenuous climbing back out.

Dad looked down. "This is a lot of steps."

"Are you thinking about the hike back up?" James asked.

"A little," Dad replied.

The family finally came to the end of the stairs. Straight ahead of them was a perfect view of a wide curtain of water crashing down to the canyon floor.

"Lower Yellowstone Falls," Dad announced. "Just look at all that water."

"Where's Upper Yellowstone Falls?" James asked.

"I believe around that bend and out of view," Dad replied.

"There are people *above* the falls!" James called out.

"I think there's a viewing area there too," Mom said.

The Parkers hung around for a few more minutes. Morgan took several photos, including one of her whole family with the falls in the background.

Lower Falls

"Shall we head up now?" Mom asked.

"I'm going to count all the steps on the way up," James informed his family. "I want to see if the sign at the top is right."

Morgan looked at James and smiled.

"What?" James asked.

"I'll tell you when we get to the top," Morgan answered.

The family began climbing the stairs.

Partway up, Dad stopped and took a deep breath. "What elevation are we at, James?" he inquired.

James thought for a second. "I think around 8,000 feet."

"No wonder this is so difficult," Dad replied.

They continued climbing the steep stairs. Every once in a while, James announced his count: "100 . . . 150 . . . 200 . . ."

Mom stopped to rest next. "The way up always seems longer," she commented.

Soon they reached the top of the metal stairs. The concrete steps weren't as steep.

"That's 300 steps so far!" James announced.

On the last step up, James stomped down on both of his feet.

"What's the official total?" Mom asked.

"Three hundred twenty-eight, exactly!" James replied.

"That's just what the sign said," Mom remembered.

"So what was that smile for, Morgan?" James asked.

"I counted the steps on the way down," Morgan replied. "But I must have missed some. I came up with just over 300."

"Should we go down again and check our count?" James asked.

Dad smiled. "I don't think so."

The Parkers walked back to the car and drove to Artist Point.

They got out of the car and approached a small group of people gathered together at the overlook.

Morgan recognized the ranger speaking to the group. "It's Tom, the geyser gazer!"

Morgan, James, Mom, and Dad stopped to listen to the final words of Tom's presentation.

"So, you see, folks," Tom explained, "in the 1800s, the western United States was thought of as a place to be tamed. People wanted to explore it, build ranches and farms, mine, log, and develop the land. Few people thought that vast areas of wilderness should be protected at all. So, in that sense, it is remarkable that a place like Yellowstone was preserved in 1872 as the world's first national park. Now," Tom built up to his conclusion, "Yellowstone is one of the last true wildernesses left. All the beauty and plants and animals that are here today were here when the first explorers arrived. And that is what the national park idea is all about: preserving fantastic places like the Grand Canyon of the Yellowstone for future generations to come."

Tom finished and the crowd clapped.

Then Tom walked up to the Parkers. "Hey, it's my geyser gazer pals."

"Are you also a ranger?" James asked.

"Only in my spare time," Tom joked. "Actually, I'm a volunteer ranger, or a VIP, as it's called. My wife and I are retired. She volunteers as a campground host while I do this. We've always dreamed of living in a place like Yellowstone. And now, we finally get to!"

"It sure is a great place," James acknowledged.

"My favorite of all the national parks," Tom stated enthusiastically. "But I can't say that Glacier, Yosemite, the Grand Canyon, Olympic, Zion, or any other park isn't as beautiful. By the way, have you seen any more geysers?"

"Lots," Morgan responded. "But we haven't always seen them erupt."

"Time and patience is all it takes," Tom stated. "But sometimes they're active even when they aren't erupting. So they're worth seeing at any time."

Another visitor walked up to Tom and asked him a question. Tom waved good-bye to the Parkers.

Morgan, James, Mom, and Dad walked up the steps to Artist Point. From there, they had views of all of the Grand Canyon of the Yellowstone.

"*Now* I see why this place is called *Yellow*stone!" James exclaimed. "Look at the yellowish color in the rocks."

"There are red and orange rocks too," Morgan pointed out. "And look at the falls!"

Other canyons may be deeper, and many canyons are longer, but no canyon in the world is quite like the Grand Canyon of the Yellowstone.

It all started with a volcanic eruption 640,000 years ago. The eruption covered the land with volcanic soil. The volcano eventually collapsed into the caldera, or giant crater, which is shown on the Yellowstone park map. Smaller eruptions and lava flows have occurred since, filling the region with volcanic rhyolite soil. Thermal features heated the rhyolite, baking it into a very weak, highly erodible material. Later, glaciers blocked water upstream from the canyon. When the glaciers melted, floodwaters wiped out the ice dam and washed away the weak soil, creating the canyon you see today. The colors in the rocks are from chemicals emitted by the thermal features in the canyon. Over time, these features cooked the rhyolite soil in the canyon. The easily eroded canyon walls expose the cooked soil to the air. This process has been "rusting" the rocks in the canyon into the colors you see today. The Grand Canyon of the Yellowstone is located in the caldera and is an active geyser basin.

The artist Thomas Moran accompanied Dr. Ferdinand V. Hayden on his 1871 expedition to Yellowstone. He sketched famous scenes in the park to document their authenticity. Some of his paintings were of Mammoth Hot Springs, Liberty Cap, Tower Falls, and the Grand Canyon of the Yellowstone.

James scanned the canyon floor with the binoculars. "There's steam coming out of several spots."

Morgan lined up her family so that Lower Falls was in the background. By then, Tom was also at the viewpoint. Morgan asked Tom if he would take their picture. She joined her family as Tom clicked the camera.

Dad looked back at the canyon once more. "I can see why people say, 'There's no canyon in the world like it.'"

Mom slowed the car. "There are bison everywhere!"

The family was driving through Hayden Valley, between the Grand Canyon of the Yellowstone and Yellowstone Lake.

One bison was right next to the road. It clomped through a dusty part of a hillside and flicked its tail back and forth.

"Its fur is so thick and matted," Mom commented.

Morgan had the window rolled down and was taking pictures. "Bison close up!" she announced.

The bison walked onto the road and stopped in front of the Parkers' car. Morgan quickly rolled up her window.

The bison stood in the middle of the road. Cars stopped on both sides.

"I don't know what to do," Mom said.

Several people got out of their cars and started creeping closer to the bison. One person had a camera with him.

The bison turned to face the approaching photographer and walked toward him. The huge beast brushed against the side of the Parkers' car, rocking it back and forth.

Suddenly, the bison charged the photographer. The man lunged behind the Parkers' car, dodging the 2,000-pound animal.

Morgan, James, Mom, and Dad watched the scene from inside their car. They sat frozen in their seats as the bison pawed the ground and turned back and forth.

The bison took a step toward the photographer again. The man moved to the opposite side of the vehicle.

Then the bison walked off the road and back into the grassy meadows.

Morgan, James, Mom, and Dad sat back and took a deep breath.

"Promise me you'll never do that," Dad said to Morgan and James.

"We promise!" Morgan and James replied in unison.

The family then watched as the man smiled, walked over to the side of the road, and laughed with some other people.

"I can't believe he's taking all of this as a joke," Mom commented.

"It's not a joke anymore," Dad said. "Look."

Two rangers came jogging up.

One ranger escorted people away from the bison and tried to get the traffic flowing. The other walked up to the man who was charged by the bison.

"I wonder what they're going to do," James said.

Mom slowly accelerated the car. They left the bison scene behind.

The road wound through Hayden Valley. To the left, the mighty Yellowstone River flowed along steadily.

Up ahead was another group of parked cars. As they approached, Morgan watched the herds of bison scattered throughout the valley. Some were close, and some were grazing in the distance.

"This looks like a scene from the Old West," Dad mentioned.

James tried to count the bison, but there were far too many. "There's got to be dozens of them," he announced.

Mom continued driving. They passed several groups of people who were stopped to take pictures of the bison herds. "At least these people are at a safe distance," James stated.

Farther up, a group of people stood on a hillside using binoculars. Mom pulled over.

"There's a ranger up there," James noticed.

All at once, everyone on the hill started walking quickly back to their cars.

The Parkers waited for the group to reach them. Dad rolled down his window as the ranger approached. "What's going on?"

"There's a grizzly out there with a bison carcass," the ranger answered. "That's an extremely dangerous situation. We can't have anyone in that area now."

"Wow!" Mom said. "We almost saw a grizzly!"

"I don't know if that's a good thing or not," Dad said.

Mom backed the car up and drove out onto the park road. A short while later, they pulled into the crowded Mud Volcano parking lot.

"The things to see here are endless!" Dad said.

DRAGON'S MOUTH SPRING
An unknown park visitor named this feature around 1912, perhaps due to the water that frequently surged from the cave like the lashing of a dragon's tongue. Until 1994, this dramatic wave-like action often splashed water as far as the boardwalk. The rumbling sounds are caused by steam and other gasses exploding through the water, causing it to crash against the walls of the hidden caverns.

"Which way?" Morgan asked.

Dad noticed a large crowd of people to the right. "How about over there?"

Then Mom clued in to what everyone saw. "Look!"

Behind the crowd was a large, steaming cavern. A sign nearby labeled it "Dragon's Mouth."

The family looked at Dragon's Mouth and listened to the thumping sounds coming from it.

Morgan gazed into the unusual cavern. "I can totally picture a dragon living in there!"

James laughed. "And he has bad sulfur breath too!"

"I think this whole area smells like rotten eggs," Mom added.

"How about we see what else is around here?" Dad suggested.

The family walked along the Mud Volcano Trail. They passed other sights, including Grizzly Fumarole, Sour Lake, and Black Dragon's Cauldron.

The Parkers stopped at Churning Cauldron.

"This one's really cooking!" Mom exclaimed. "The water is boiling like crazy."

Morgan took pictures. "It's hard to get a good shot with all the steam."

Suddenly, a child screamed.

A moment later, a man with a panicked look on his face carried a shrieking boy down the boardwalk. The boy had a sweatshirt wrapped around his leg.

Dad watched the injured child being whisked away. "I wonder if he got burned."

"I was afraid to look," James admitted.

"We just have to stay on the trail," Mom said.

They somberly returned to their car and drove to the campground across from Yellowstone Lake.

Later that evening, the family sat at the back of the campground amphitheater. A blanket was draped over the four of them.

James felt the park bench next to him. "It's icy."

WARM DAYS, COOL NIGHTS

Campers and hikers in Yellowstone should be prepared for wintry weather at any time of the year. Many warm summer days turn into stormy afternoons with rain, wind, hail, thunder, and lightning. Summer days are often in the seventies, but nights are cold, with temperatures dropping into the thirties and sometimes even the twenties. Frost and freezing conditions are not unusual. Always bring rain gear and warm clothes when hiking and backpacking in Yellowstone—even if it is warm and dry when you leave.

They were listening to a ranger talking about bison. "At one point, only twenty-three bison were still alive out of the original 60 million. Those twenty-three were here in Yellowstone."

"We're lucky we saw so many, then," Morgan whispered to Mom.

The ranger continued. "Now, thanks to places like Yellowstone and laws like the Endangered Species Act, there are several thousand bison living in the park."

Bison are the largest land mammals in North America. Male bison can weigh over 2,000 pounds, which is almost twice as much as a Holstein cow.

Bison, which are sometimes called buffalo, once lived throughout the North American continent. It was said that there were "seas of buffalo across the plains."

The demise of the bison in North America began with fur traders hunting them. Later, people on wagon trains killed bison for meat and sport. Railroad workers also killed bison for food as they completed track lines out West. Hunters swarmed the plains, killing as many bison as they could and sometimes taking only the tongue, which was considered a delicacy. Some famous "buffalo runners," including Buffalo Bill Cody, claimed to have killed up to 4,000 bison on their own. Additionally, railroad passengers were asked to shoot bison from train windows. This was done to cut off the Indians' food supply. Millions of bison were left to rot on the plains.

All of these events combined to reduce the bison population to around 200. But further poaching occurred. Eventually, the last twenty-three hid out in Pelican Valley in Yellowstone. The Lacey Act stopped further slaughter of these bison, and later the Endangered Species Act protected any species of plant or animal whose population was in danger.

Currently there are about 3,500 to 4,000 bison living in Yellowstone.

WHERE THE BUFFALO ROAM

"So," the ranger concluded, "please continue to help the bison. You can do this by enjoying them from a distance and by not driving over the speed limit. We had two bison hit by cars and killed recently in the park.

Finally, learn as much as you can about the park and its wild features. Thank you for coming."

The audience clapped.

Mom, Dad, Morgan, and James got up. They turned their flashlights on and strolled back to their campsite. A full moon was shining over massive Yellowstone Lake.

Dad looked out over the vast, moonlit, calm waters. "Every part of this park is so different."

They quickly brushed their teeth and got into their tent. Mom turned on the battery-operated lantern. Dad looked at Morgan and James, who were already snug in their sleeping bags. "No cards tonight, I guess, right?"

Morgan looked up at Dad. "Aren't you freezing?"

"You're right," Dad replied. "I'm going to get into my sleeping bag too. It is cold."

• • •

James woke up first the next morning. He fumbled around until he found his journal. James wrote:

This is James Parker reporting.

I now know what I want to be when I grow up. A park ranger! What a great job. You get to live at one of the most beautiful places in the world, teach people about it, and help protect the park and the wildlife living in it. I wonder what subjects I'll have to study, though? Geology, like Dad? And Mom majored in botany in college. It all seems so interesting to me.

Speaking of parks, Yellowstone is an incredible one. And, so far, we've seen tons of animals, including bison, elk, pronghorn, moose, bighorn sheep, and a black bear. My wildlife map is getting very crowded! Now I expect to see wildlife every day.

There are endless places to explore here: more geysers, lakes, hikes, and . . .

Anyway, more adventures from Yellowstone soon.

James Parker

Morgan opened her eyes and saw James writing. "I need to get caught up too."

Morgan got dressed and put on a jacket, a cap, and gloves.

"You look like you're going skiing!" James exclaimed.

Morgan smiled and then quickly slipped outside. A white blanket of frost covered the area around the campground. Morgan put a towel down on the picnic table bench and began writing.

Dear Diary,

It's cold. The thermometer attached to my jacket reads 29 degrees! There's ice everywhere. And my hands are freezing. Isn't it supposed to be summer?

Anyway, yesterday was such an interesting day. But what I remember most was the crying child being rushed out of the Mud Volcano area. What happened to him? Did he get burned or hurt by an animal? I can imagine both things happening in Yellowstone. Then there was that person who got chased by the bison because he got too close.

People need to listen to the rules. They're here for your own safety. Rule #1: Don't get too close to an animal to take a picture. Rule #2: Stay off the hot soil near geysers. Rule #3: Anyway, you get my point.

Well, I can hear Mom and Dad stirring inside their igloo. And James and I promised we'd make breakfast today. At least the sun is starting to finally peek through the trees.

Thawing out in Yellowstone,

Morgan

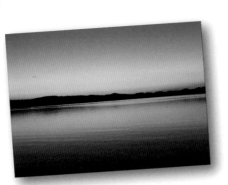

Tom scanned the people gathered at the Storm Point

trailhead. "I need a couple of young volunteers."

Morgan and James raised their hands.

"Hey, it's my two buddies! Come on up!"

The crowd looked at Morgan and James. Dad smiled. "I guess you're the chosen ones."

Morgan and James walked up to Tom. Tom had them introduce themselves. Then Tom took Morgan and James away from the group. He got their props ready and quietly gave them some instructions. Then the three of them returned to face the crowd.

"Right here," Tom began, "magma shot up through the Earth's crust."

James propelled a piece of red cardboard up through another piece of broken cardboard that represented the Earth's surface.

"Where all of you are standing now is exactly where the world's largest volcano erupted 640,000 years ago," Tom explained. "It was an eruption a thousand times greater than the Mt. Saint Helens eruption in 1980. The hot plume of magma that created this volcano is still under us now. And, it's awfully close. The Earth's crust is only one to three miles thick here. The worldwide average is more than forty-five miles."

Morgan showed two models of the Earth's crust. One was of Yellowstone's thin layer. The other was of a much thicker layer representing other parts of the world.

Tom continued. "After this eruption, the volcano collapsed."
James showed a model of the area buckling.

"And that's what we're standing on today," Tom concluded. "A collapsed volcano called a caldera and the most active thermal area in the world. Morgan will now show you the caldera area on the park map."

Morgan held up a Yellowstone map for everyone to see. She pointed out the large round area representing the caldera.

"Let's give a big hand to our two volunteers here," Tom said.

The audience clapped while Morgan and James walked back to Mom and Dad.

"And one other thing before we start our hike," Tom added. "Please be careful near any thermal features and stay on the marked path. We had a child get burned yesterday at the Mud Volcano area."

"That must have been who we saw!" Morgan said.

"So," Tom stated enthusiastically, "follow me to Storm Point."

"Are there any bears out here?" a person asked.

"Oh, yeah," Tom replied. "If we see a bear, the best thing to do is form a tight circle, and put me in the middle!"

The crowd laughed.

"But, really, with such a large group like this, we should be fine," Tom said. "Although I almost guarantee we will

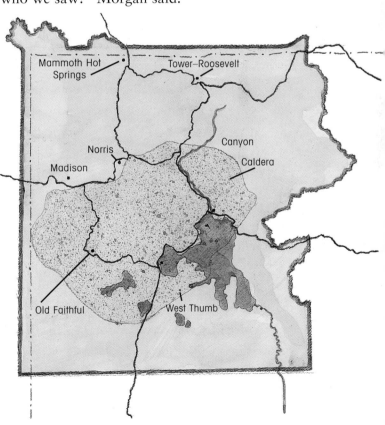

see other animals. Come on," Tom directed, "to one of my favorite places in the park."

The group of visitors began walking. After a while, they approached a small hill.

Tom stopped and waited for everyone to gather together. "At the top of this hill," he explained, "we're likely to see two different types of animals. Just stay quiet. We'll be a safe distance away, so there's no need to worry."

Everyone climbed the hill and immediately saw a large pile of jumbled rocks. "Look!" Morgan called out softly.

A marmot was perched on one of the rocks. It stood up on its hind legs and sniffed the air nervously.

"That's the sentry of the marmot colony," Tom whispered. "Has anyone seen the other animals yet?"

"Over there!" a person pointed out.

To the far right, a couple of animals were lounging around in the dirt and flicking their ears back and forth. One started licking its paw.

"They look like dogs," Morgan said.

"Or wolves," James added.

"They're coyotes," Tom informed the group. "And here in Yellowstone, our coyotes are larger than anywhere else in North America."

"How many of them are there?" Morgan asked.

"About a half dozen," Tom replied. "How many have all of you seen so far?"

"Only two," someone answered.

"Wait. There's a third one!" Dad announced.

The third coyote was sneaking up on the rock pile. The coyote squatted behind a rock and quietly crept closer to the marmot colony.

"It's hunting," Morgan realized.

Suddenly, the coyote lunged. It grabbed onto the back of the sentry marmot's neck and lifted it off the rock. The marmot squealed and kicked its legs around erratically.

Morgan closed her eyes. "I can't look."

The coyote trotted away with its prey and headed back to the pack. Along the way, it dropped the marmot on the ground. The marmot weakly flung its paws and tried to right itself. The coyote nuzzled the marmot back over and bit into it more firmly. Then it walked toward the trees.

Tom looked at the group. "Well, you don't get to see that every day!"

"Where's it going with it?" James asked.

"There's a den back there and a family to feed," Tom answered. "Come on, everyone. There's more to show you."

The group followed Tom along the trail.

Tom walked ahead to an area overlooking Yellowstone Lake. He stood up on a rock and announced, "Welcome to Storm Point. This spot was named by the Hayden party of explorers who were out here during a thunderstorm. We call Yellowstone Lake an inland ocean. That's because of its size. This is the largest lake at this elevation in the lower forty-eight states. And, Yellowstone Lake is home to the largest population of cutthroat trout in the world. It's the perfect habitat for them."

Tom held up the park map. "If you look on the map, you can see that much of this lake is in the caldera area. There's more than just a lake out there. Studies indicate that the most active geyser basin in the park is underneath it.

"And one other thing," Tom continued. "See Stevenson Island out there? A few years ago, two young grizzlies were stuck on that island. Does anyone have any idea how they got there?"

The group looked at Tom eagerly.

"Well," Tom finished, "Yellowstone Lake freezes over in winter. Apparently, when the lake was iced over, a mother grizzly walked out there with her two cubs. When the lake thawed out in the springtime, the mother swam back and left the cubs behind. We discovered the grizzlies because boat tours saw them on the island. A group of rangers went out there and trapped the bears and brought them back to the mainland. They were old enough to be on their own at that point anyway.

"Enough of my stories," Tom said. "Please enjoy Storm Point, and in a little while, we'll continue on our way."

The Parkers sat on the rocks overlooking the lake.

The group hung around a few more minutes. Then Tom said, "Let's get going, everyone. I need to get you back to your cars now."

The Parkers and the other hikers followed Tom through a more forested part of the trail. Eventually they were all back to their cars at the trailhead.

"I'm glad we went on that walk," Dad said to James and Morgan. "It was neat to learn more about Yellowstone's geology, especially from you two."

"And from Tom," Morgan added.

Morgan, James, Mom, and Dad stood on top of a bluff.

They could see all the way down to Heart Lake, where they would camp for the next two nights. Massive Mt. Sheridan, with its fire tower on top, was to their right.

"What a great way to end our trip," Dad said, "backpacking in Yellowstone."

"I agree," Mom added. "The Yellowstone backcountry wilderness awaits."

Morgan noticed a pink mud hole near the top of the hill. "Look at that!"

The mud pot was belching up pink splats of mud. Other holes nearby were steaming, boiling, and hissing.

"Even way out here, the Yellowstone show goes on," Dad commented.

They hiked the last three miles down to Heart Lake. Along the way, they passed pools of steaming water.

"Just some more examples of the over 10,000 thermal features in Yellowstone," Dad said. "It makes me feel like we aren't on planet Earth."

They came to a small footbridge. Witch Creek flowed steadily underneath it. Mom knelt down to touch the water. "Warm," she informed her family, "like a hot bath."

As they approached the lake, they saw a backcountry ranger cabin.

"Quite a job to be stationed out here for the summer," Mom stated.

Dad pointed to a bunch of scratches and claw marks outside the cabin. "Maybe it isn't that fun. Look at these!"

"Are you thinking what I'm thinking?" James asked.

"Yes, if you think those are from a bear," Dad replied.

James looked at the bear-spray canisters clipped on Mom and Dad's belts. "That's what I was thinking."

The trail veered to the right, following the shoreline of Heart Lake. A side trail led to the top of Mt. Sheridan.

A little more than a mile past the ranger cabin, a small sign next to the trail read 8H3 + 8H2.

"Here's our home for the next two nights," Mom announced.

Mom led the way toward their site. She pointed to a wooden pole that was secured high above the ground between two trees. "There's the bear pole."

A short distance away they found a flat tent area with a view overlooking Heart Lake.

"We couldn't have a prettier site," Dad said.

Morgan, James, Mom, and Dad set up camp. They pitched their tent on the flat spot and put on warm clothes. As evening set in, they cooked dinner at the fire pit near the bear pole.

"It's quiet out here," Morgan noticed.

"I love it!" Dad said. "Along with that sound of running water. Which reminds me, I'm going to go filter some water from the creek before dark."

Dad took four bottles and the filter over to the nearby stream. He crossed a little footbridge that led to a small, clear pool of water.

James, Morgan, and Mom put all their food and cooking gear into their packs and changed clothes. "To make sure you don't bring any food scent into the tent," Mom explained.

While Dad filtered, he saw a family cooking at the campsite next to theirs.

Dad waved to the family.

The father waved back.

Dad noticed a couple of fishing rods leaning against the trees.

After filtering, Dad walked over to chat with the family.

Meanwhile, Morgan, James, and Mom hoisted their packs high up on the bear pole and tied them securely. It was nearly dark when Dad returned.

"We were wondering about you," Morgan said.

"There's a nice family camped across the creek," Dad said. "It's good to have some other people nearby, I think."

Morgan, James, and Mom climbed into the tent. Under the darkened skies, Dad stood outside for a moment. He scanned the wooded area near camp, the distant slopes up Mt. Sheridan, and peaceful Heart Lake. Finally, Dad changed clothes and hung the worn ones in a sack alongside the backpacks. Then Dad joined his family inside.

Once they were all snug in their sleeping bags, the Parkers fell asleep to the sounds of the wilderness night.

. . .

"Ow . . . ow . . . owwwwww!"

Several hours later, howling started.

Morgan heard it first. Her heart beat quickly as she listened.

"Ow . . . ow!"

"Is anyone awake?" Morgan whispered.

"I am," Mom answered.

"Owww . . . owww . . ."

Dad sat up. "Those are wolves!"

"I'm getting goose bumps just listening to them," James said.

The howling continued. Morgan scooted closer to her parents. "It's spooky sounding."

"I certainly agree with that," Dad said. "But it's also pretty cool. Having packs of wolves roaming about in Yellowstone is one of the greatest wildlife recovery stories ever."

After being gone for more than fifty years, wolves have returned to Yellowstone. In 1995 and 1996, thirty-one gray wolves were released in the park. Now there are about 120 wolves living in Yellowstone, although the number fluctuates yearly.

Wolves eat mostly elk, but will occasionally eat deer and younger or older bison, which are easier to prey upon.

Yellowstone visitors see wolves nearly every day. There are even guided groups that go out and look for wolves in places such as the Lamar Valley. Wolf watching is now one of the most popular activities in the park.

James moved closer to Mom and Dad too. "I wouldn't worry about them," Mom reassured. "They're a long way off, and they certainly aren't interested in us."

After a while, the howling faded. "They must be wandering away," Mom said.

Morgan, James, Mom, and Dad slowly fell back to sleep.

Mom opened the tent window.

"It's nice to have daylight back," James commented.

Mom smiled. "I know what you mean."

The Parkers got up. They walked over to the cooking area.

Morgan looked up at their dangling backpacks. "Everything looks the same as when we left it."

One by one, they untied and lowered their packs to eye level. They washed their hands with water from the bottles and pulled out food for the day. Dad started preparing oatmeal. James made peanut butter sand-wiches. Mom and Morgan grabbed the water bottles and filter and headed for the stream.

Mom stopped. A large pile of scat was just off the path. "Whoa. That looks like it's from a bear."

"How do you know?" Morgan asked.

"Just by the size of it, and that bears eat so many different things," Mom replied. "This scat has fur and berries in it."

Immediately, Mom and Morgan looked around. They didn't see any bears. Then Mom realized she wasn't carrying her bear spray.

"Come on, Morgan," Mom said. "We can't filter water right now."

Morgan and Mom turned around and walked back to camp. Mom grabbed her bear spray, then looked at Dad. "Can I show you some-thing, Robert?"

Dad heard the seriousness in Mom's voice. "Of course."

"Get your bear spray first," Mom directed. "And James, you come with us too, okay?"

Mom and Morgan walked Dad and James over to the pile of scat.

"Was this here yesterday?" Mom asked Dad.

Dad looked at the scat. "I walked this exact path to the stream last night. I think I would have noticed it. But it was almost dark, so I can't be sure."

"It doesn't look that fresh," Mom said.

"Was it a black bear or a grizzly?" James asked nervously.

Mom put her hand on James's shoulder. "That is something we just can't tell by scat."

Dad looked across the small creek. In the distance, he saw the family he had met the day before, now tearing down their camp. Dad looked at Mom. "I'm going to go and talk with them for a minute. I'll take my spray with me. I'll be right back, okay?"

Mom nodded. "We'll be getting ready for the day. Hurry. Be quick."

"I'll be just a minute," Dad said seriously.

Morgan, James, and Mom walked back to their cooking area. Meanwhile, Dad crossed the small bridge and walked up to the family. "Good morning," he greeted them.

"Good morning," the father replied.

"Did you see a bear around last night?" Dad asked.

The father shook his head. "No."

Dad told the family about the scat. "Are you heading out today?"

"Yes," the mother answered. "We only reserved our campsite for last night."

Dad gestured toward the fishing rods. "Are you going to do any fishing?"

"Definitely," the father answered. "Before we go."

"Where's a good fishing spot?" Dad inquired.

"Actually," the father replied, "the ranger told us right here, where this stream runs into Heart Lake."

"Really?" Dad replied.

"So," the mother explained, "my husband and older son are going to fish while my other son and I climb Mt. Sheridan. We'll all meet at the junction this afternoon at 3:00 p.m. and hike out together."

Dad nodded. "That sounds like a great plan."

The older boy smiled. "Do you want to join us?"

"You've got me thinking," Dad replied. "Can you come over to our site on the way out?"

"Sure," the boy answered.

Dad walked back and explained his idea to Morgan, James, and Mom.

"It'll give me a chance to fish for a few hours," Dad said.

"And I really want to hike to the top of that mountain," Mom said.

"I want to go fishing!" Morgan exclaimed.

"Me too," James added.

Dad looked at his children. "What do you think?" he asked Mom.

"I think the three of you will be fine," Mom answered. "And I'll be hiking with two other people, so we'll all be in a group."

"How about this?" Dad added. "We'll meet you at the trailhead to Mt. Sheridan at 3:00 p.m. to accompany you back."

"I appreciate that," Mom said. "But it's only a half mile or so back to here on the main trail. I'll be fine."

Dad gave Mom a concerned look. "Okay," he reluctantly agreed.

The other family walked over to the Parkers' campsite.

The father introduced his family. "I'm Mark and this is my wife, Catherine. Our younger son, Troy, is going hiking. Our older son, Vincent, wants to fish. Anyway, we're the Alexander clan, or what's left of it," Mark finished. "Our two daughters have grown up and moved away."

Mark and Vincent looked at Dad. Dad nodded back in recognition.

"Is it okay if we hang our two packs up here with yours while we fish?" Mark asked. "We don't know if someone's going to move into our site soon or not."

"Of course," Dad replied.

"You've got your bear spray, right?" Dad asked Mom.

Mom pointed to her belt. "And I can see yours is ready too."

Dad kissed Mom good-bye.

"Have fun hiking," James said.

"Bye, Mom," Morgan added.

Mom took off with Catherine and Troy. The three of them hiked back to the main trail and turned right. They disappeared over a small hill. Dad got out the fishing rods. Then he tied on some flies.

Mark and Vincent also prepared their rods. A moment later, the five of them tramped down to the water.

Dad helped James and Morgan get started. He watched them cast their flies onto the lake. "Snap your elbow or wrist when you let the line go," Dad instructed. "That will give you more distance in your cast."

After a while, Dad cast his line and let his fly gracefully touch the surface of Heart Lake. Then he inched his line in.

Dad looked at his surroundings. The surface of the water was calm. A mirror image of the mountains and forest nearby was reflected in the lake's waters.

"It's a perfect morning!" Dad announced.

"That it is," Mark responded. "That it is."

. . .

Mom, Catherine, and Troy reached the Mt. Sheridan Trail junction. Catherine and Troy tied up their packs on the bear pole nearby. Once they finished, they headed up the trail to Mt. Sheridan.

They stayed close together and kept a steady pace for their assault of the summit.

Mom, Catherine, and Troy continued climbing.

They talked and made noise along the trail, hoping to not surprise any bears that might be nearby. The path to the summit zigzagged through the forest, eventually heading up into more-open areas.

Two backcountry rangers heading down the mountain passed them on the trail.

"Hello," one of them greeted Mom's group. "You're doing great, you're almost there."

"Thanks," Catherine said back.

The two rangers quickly hiked down and were soon out of sight.

The trail reached over 10,000 feet in elevation. The bushes and trees were sparse, short, and stunted by the weather. There were meadows full of wildflowers. A patch of snow still clung to a cirque, or circular-shaped area created by a glacier, near the top of the mountain.

I wish Dad and the twins were seeing this, Mom thought.

• • •

"Why don't we move to a new spot?" Dad suggested. "The fish must be spooked in this area by now anyway."

"They probably heard us talking," James said.

"Come over here first," Dad said.

Morgan and James walked over to Dad. Dad showed them his collection of flies. "Do you want to try a different one?"

"How about the one with stripes?" Morgan asked.

"I like that one too," James said.

"Ah, the old favorite—guaranteed to catch a fish!" Dad exclaimed proudly. "And I happen to have two of them!"

Dad helped Morgan and James tie on their flies. They walked a short distance to a new spot on the lake and cast their lines.

Dad heard a splash. He turned to see Morgan's rod bending over.

Morgan looked at Dad. "Pull the rod back quickly!" Dad called out.

Morgan reeled her line in. The fish tried to swim away, bending Morgan's rod over farther. Morgan continued to reel in the fish. She walked into the water and approached it.

Morgan saw the rainbow-colored trout dash back and forth in the water. She held her rod tightly as the fish continued to fight. Morgan reeled in the line some more. She lifted her line out of the water, but the fish slipped off the hook and plopped back into the lake.

Morgan looked at James and Dad disappointedly.

Dad walked over and shrugged his shoulders. "That's happened to me many times. Next time you get a bite, though, yank on the line hard to really hook it. Otherwise, the fish spit the hook out when they realize it isn't food."

"At least you had one!" James said.

"Well, we're supposed to release the fish anyway," Morgan said. "I just let it go early."

Dad laughed. "Very true."

. . .

Mom, Catherine, and Troy climbed a steep section of the trail. They stopped to rest a moment and look out at the view.

"Hey, I think that group of trees down there is where we're camped," Catherine pointed out.

"Look!" Mom exclaimed.

Two large brown animals with enormous curled horns on their heads were under the trees just off the trail.

"Wow," Catherine whispered. "Bighorns!"

"We're so close to them," Mom said.

The bighorns were casually grazing. They seemed to not pay attention to the group.

"I wish my whole family was seeing this," Mom said.

"Mine too," Catherine added.

"Can you see our fishermen?" Mom asked.

"The trees are in the way," Troy responded.

Mom pointed out where the two bodies of water were separated by a peninsula of land. "I can see now why it's called Heart Lake."

They came to a knife-edged ridge. A steep drop-off covered by loose rock next to the trail led to what would be a long fall. One by one, Mom, Catherine, and Troy carefully walked across the ridge.

They regathered at the top and continued hiking. The fire tower was just up ahead.

• • •

Dad, James, and Morgan continued fishing. A small, sleek, black head of an animal broke through the surface of the water and swam along.

James watched the animal. Suddenly, it dove underwater. James looked around for a few seconds but didn't see it come back up. Then the animal resurfaced a short distance away with a small fish in its mouth. The fish wiggled back and forth, trying to escape its captor.

"An otter!" James realized, and Dad laughed. "He's a heck of a lot better at fishing than we are!"

The otter flipped the fish up and swallowed it in one gulp. Then it swam quickly away.

. . .

A man stood on the porch of the fire lookout on Mt. Sheridan. A pair of binoculars dangled around his neck.

"Greetings!" he said. "How was the climb?"

"Pretty grueling," Troy replied.

"My name's Bill," the man introduced himself. "Feel free to look around, and let me know if you need anything."

Mom noticed dish soap near the window inside. "Do you live here?"

Bill smiled. "Yes. For many, many summers."

"Wow," Mom said. "Your house has the best view I've ever seen."

"But I'm also here to watch for and report fires," Bill said.

After walking around the summit, Mom, Catherine, and Troy gathered around as Bill told them a story.

"I wasn't up here during the 1988 fires," Bill said. "But I have seen my share of lightning strikes and smaller fires. One time I could actually feel the electricity in the air. My hair was standing on end. I ran into the fire tower and saw lightning hit a tree nearby. The thunder was unbelievable. But the tower didn't get hit, and I was reasonably safe inside anyway. Fortunately, there was a lot of rain with that thunderstorm, so the fires that day were naturally squelched."

Bill smiled. "Yeah, I can tell life-in-the-fire-tower stories all day."

Mom signed the logbook and read comments from other visitors. "People from all over the world have come here," she realized.

Mom, Catherine, and Troy thanked Bill, then began their climb back down the mountain.

. . .

Mark and Vincent walked along the lake toward Dad, James, and Morgan.

"It's 2:00 p.m.," Mark announced. "We're going to head over early and make lunch for Catherine and Troy."

Dad, Morgan, and James sloshed out of the shallow water and walked back to their campsite. They watched Mark and Vincent get their backpacks down from the bear pole.

"You sure you don't want to come with us?" Mark offered.

"We're going to fish a bit more then head up to meet Mom along the trail," Dad answered.

Morgan, James, and Dad said good-bye.

Mark and Vincent took off hiking and disappeared over a small hill.

The Parkers grabbed their fishing rods. Something snapped in the bushes. Dad looked around. His pulse quickened.

Dad took a deep breath and let out a gush of air. "Boy, your thoughts can sure get the best of you quickly out here."

Dad looked at the lake and then at Morgan and James. "Do you want to fish some more or head out to get Mom?"

"Can we try fishing a few more minutes?" Morgan asked. "It would be nice to at least catch something."

Something cracked in the bushes again. Morgan, James, and Dad looked around but didn't see anything.

Dad remembered the bear warning sign near Mystic Falls. *There's no guarantee of your safety* kept ringing through his head.

Something cracked in the woods again.

Dad looked around nervously. "Maybe we should go meet Mom now," he suggested.

They heard a loud, huffing sound.

Dad dropped his fishing rod and looked up.

The sound came again from about thirty feet away, behind the trees. Only this time it sounded more like a deep, guttural snort. Dad turned to see a large bear lumbering toward the three of them.

Dad grabbed James and Morgan. He reached for his bear spray, popped the safety latch, and put his finger on the nozzle.

Dad looked at the bear. It had a dish-shaped face, short, rounded ears, and a hump between its shoulders. The bear was cinnamon-colored. *An adult grizzly!* Dad realized.

The grizzly stopped. It turned back and forth several times then stood up on its hind legs while looking at James, Morgan, and Dad. Then the grizzly dropped down on all four feet.

Dad held on to his two children and backed up a few feet. "Don't look at its eyes," he directed calmly. "And don't run. But be ready to do exactly what I tell you to."

The grizzly snorted and shuffled his feet. Then the bear charged straight at Dad, James, and Morgan.

. . .

Mom, Catherine, and Troy hiked quickly down the mountain. "Going down is sure a lot easier than going up," Mom commented.

They came to the bear pole near the bottom of the trail. Mark and Vincent were already there, taking down the two backpacks.

"Hi!" Catherine said to her husband.

"Hey there," Mark replied. "How was the hike?"

"Fantastic," Troy answered. "The views were amazing. And this guy, Bill, lives up there in the fire lookout."

"Sounds like I missed something special," Mark stated.

"How's my family?" Mom asked.

"Fine," Mark answered. "I think they wanted to try fishing a little longer before coming to get you."

"That's not a surprise," Mom stated. Then she said good-bye to the family and started walking back to the campsite.

• • •

Morgan cowered behind Dad. James cringed and gripped his father.

Dad aimed the spray at the bear.

The grizzly stopped charging twenty feet before reaching them. The bear paced back and forth, snorting and huffing. It breathed heavily and made clicking sounds with its jaw.

Suddenly, the grizzly charged again.

Dad pushed the lever of the bear spray. A loud hissing sound came from the canister as an orange fog spewed into the air toward the grizzly. Some of the spray hit a tree. The bear kept charging.

Dad pulled James and Morgan closer. "Drop!" he commanded.

Morgan, James, and Dad fell to the ground. Dad lost hold of the bear-spray canister. He put his hands over the back of Morgan and James's heads and held them tightly against him. "Don't move!" Dad said urgently. The three of them had their faces toward the ground.

The grizzly came right up to them. It nudged them with its nose and used its paws to try and roll each of them over. Dad kept his hands and arms wrapped tightly around Morgan and James. His heart beat wildly.

The bear must realize we're not dead, Dad thought.

The bear pawed around at Morgan, James, and Dad a few times. It nudged at them with its nose once more then finally walked away.

"Stay still," Dad whispered. His mind raced. How far away is the bear? Should we get up now? Dad silently counted to ten, then twenty. He didn't hear anything. Then Dad counted some more.

Slowly, Dad began to move his arm, hoping to grab the bear spray.

The bear lumbered back and stood next to Dad. It nudged the three of them again, trying to turn them over.

Dad continued to hold his arms over Morgan and James and kept as still as possible. Morgan tried to stop herself from shaking.

The standoff with the bear continued for several more minutes. But to Dad, Morgan, and James, it seemed like a lifetime; everything was happening in slow motion.

The bear wandered away again. Dad waited and listened. He slowly moved his hand toward the bear spray. This time, he grabbed it. Dad held up the spray. He turned his head to see which way the nozzle was pointed.

Slowly, Dad began to peel himself off the ground. "Stay down for now," he instructed. Dad lifted his body to his knees and cautiously looked around. He held the bear spray out and readied himself to either be attacked or to shoot the repellent.

Dad heard a deep grunt behind him, followed by charging footsteps. Dad whirled around and fired.

The bear was ten feet away and lunging when the spray connected.

The powerful, noxious mist blasted the bear's face. The grizzly froze in its tracks. It bellowed loudly then shook its head violently. The bear sneezed several times and rubbed its face into the ground, stirring up a small cloud of dust. Then it spun around and crashed off into the woods.

Dad stood up. "Get up now!" he commanded. "We have to get out of here!"

Immediately, Dad began taking down all the backpacks. Once the ropes were untied, he gave James and Morgan their packs and held onto Mom's. Dad threw the looped rope around his neck.

"We're heading out to get Mom as quickly as possible. We can't stay here, and I don't want her alone on the trail with that grizzly around."

Morgan, James, and Dad got out of camp as fast as they could. Dad slipped and fell on a wet mossy area and then sprang to his feet again, looking for the bear.

Dad saw it in the distance. The grizzly was rambling away while still violently shaking its head and pawing at its eyes and face.

I wonder how long that will last, Dad thought.

Morgan, James, and Dad scrambled back to the main trail. "You two go first, and I'll be right behind you," Dad instructed. They took off for the Mt. Sheridan trailhead. At the top of the first hill, Dad turned around to look, but the grizzly was no longer in sight.

"How are you two doing?" Dad asked James and Morgan. "Did the bear hurt you?"

James and Morgan both shook their heads no.

Morgan, James, and Dad walked as fast as they could.

"There's Mom!" James called out and waved. Mom waved back, and then stopped. *Why do they have all our backpacks?* she thought. *And why is Dad carrying the rope?*

Mom watched Dad and the twins run frantically toward her. The bear spray was in Dad's hand. Mom took off and ran toward Dad.

A moment later, they met.

Morgan and James hugged Mom and started crying. Dad dropped Mom's pack and grabbed onto her. After a moment, Dad calmed down enough to tell Mom about the grizzly.

"Are you okay? Are you okay?" Mom kept asking.

Dad gasped, then finally answered. "We're okay. It never really attacked us."

Mom looked at their backpacks and toward where they were camped. "We have to go back," she realized. "Our tent and sleeping bags are still there."

Morgan, James, and Dad looked at each other. "We forgot about that," James said.

The Parkers stood in silence for a moment.

"When we go back there, we'll stay together," Dad announced. "And we'll get out of there as fast as possible."

Morgan, James, Mom, and Dad marched like nervous soldiers back into battle. Dad led the way.

They walked over a small hill. Up ahead was the turnoff to their campsite. James stopped. "I don't want to go back in there!" he protested.

"Me either," Morgan added.

Dad put his arms around his children. "I wish we didn't have to."

"Can't James and I just wait here?" Morgan pleaded.

"I'm scared too," Mom stated. "But we can't leave you two out here if there's a grizzly around. You have to come with us."

The family reluctantly headed back to their campsite.

They arrived at the tent and immediately packed up their sleeping bags, mattresses, and everything else inside. They stuffed their gear haphazardly into their backpacks. Mom and Dad kept searching the area with their bear spray out and ready to use.

"I can't believe we forgot about all this," Morgan said. "I didn't even notice how light my pack was."

The Parkers did one more quick check of the campsite then dashed toward the main trail.

Dad wrinkled his nose and sniffed the air. "Wait here a second," he said. He tromped into the grass off the trail. After walking about fifty feet, Dad stopped and peered into the brush. He held his hand up to his

face, took a quick breath of air, and hurried back to his family.

"I thought I smelled something funny," he informed them. "And now I know why that bear was so upset."

"What was it?" Mom asked.

"A partially eaten deer," Dad replied. "We really need to hustle out of here now!"

"A carcass," James recalled. He remembered the ranger sending everyone back to their cars in Hayden Valley.

"Come on!" Dad hurried his family along.

Once back on the main trail, Mom went first and Dad stayed in back. Both carried their bear spray in their hands.

The Parkers focused their energy on getting a large distance away from the campsite. They walked as fast as they could.

They passed the Mt. Sheridan Trail junction. Finally, Morgan, James, Mom, and Dad slowed down a bit.

"What was it like being so close to a grizzly?" Mom asked.

"The scariest moment of my life," Morgan answered. "My hands are still shaking."

"I felt it brush its nose against me," James informed her. "And it smelled awful."

Dad led them toward the ranger's cabin. "It's a relief to see some sort of connection to civilization," he said.

Dad walked right up to the door of the cabin and saw the claw marks. "I wonder if these are from the same bear," he said.

Dad pounded his fist against the door and listened. There was no sound inside.

"I saw two backcountry rangers on the Mt. Sheridan Trail earlier today," Mom said. "So at least they're around."

Dad took off his pack and leaned it against the cabin. There was a stinging pain near his shoulder, but he tried to ignore it. Dad touched the back of his shirt and felt a tear. He took a deep breath.

we ought to get some food in us now," Mom suggested. She grabbed the trail mix from her pack and passed it around.

Dad checked his watch. "It's four o'clock," he announced. "How far is it to the car, James?"

"Eight miles," James recalled.

"What do you think?" Dad asked Mom. "We have about five hours of daylight left. That's enough time to get back to the trailhead before dark. I'd rather do that than wait here and hike out in the morning."

"Are you up for eight miles of hiking now?" Mom asked the twins.

"I am," Morgan answered.

"It's better than camping out here," James added.

"I think we should go for it," Dad concluded. "Can I borrow a piece of paper from your journal?" he asked Morgan.

Morgan found her journal and tore off a sheet of paper. "And a pen," Dad added.

Dad took the pen and paper and quickly jotted down a note for the ranger. He slipped it into a crack in the door. "Come on, let's get out of here."

Morgan, James, Mom, and Dad took off.

"What did you write?" James asked.

"I told them what happened and to not let anyone camp in 8H3 and 8H2," Dad answered. "And gave them our plans so they know what we are doing."

"Good idea," Mom said, feeling a bit relieved.

They zipped past the meadows and began climbing along Witch Creek. Meanwhile, clouds had built up, blocking the late afternoon sun.

Soon it started raining.

Mom fished through her backpack for ponchos. She handed one to Dad, Morgan, and James. "We should put these on."

The Parkers continued climbing. Rain splatted down. Several rounds of thunder rumbled in the distance.

Suddenly, lightning split the sky ahead of them. Thunder instantly cracked the air.

"Whoa!" Mom froze and looked at the sky.

It started to hail. First, a few pea-sized specks of ice splattered down. Then the hail got larger. Before long, marble-sized ice balls showered all around and bounced off the trail.

Lightning flashed again. Thunder echoed instantly.

"Up ahead!" Mom directed. She raced her family into the middle of a small grove of lodgepole pines. Morgan, James, Mom, and Dad scooted into the trees for cover.

To their surprise, the family ran into the Alexanders. They were sitting on a downed log with a large tarp draped over their heads. The Alexanders made room for the Parkers. In a moment, both families were scrunched together under the tarp. Meanwhile, rain and hail pounded down.

"I guess there's no rest for the weary," Dad said. He told the Alexanders about the grizzly.

The hail let up. Dad peeked out from under the dripping tarp and scanned the skies. "It looks like it's clearing," he reported. "I think the sun will be out soon too. We should press on."

The families got out from under the tarp.

. . .

The Parkers trekked up the ridge, with the Alexanders right behind them.

Morgan pointed toward the mountains. "Look!" A veil of white was drifting across the sky and heading their way. It sounded like an approaching train.

Mom saw the sheets of hail coming. "I think we have about twenty seconds to take cover again," she called out.

They quickly headed for another small group of trees. The Parkers huddled together as the first few hailstones plunked down.

The Alexander family walked past them. "We're going to try and press on," Mark informed the Parkers.

Hailstones popped down everywhere. They bounced all around and quickly piled up on the ground. It hailed for several minutes. Then, just as fast as the hail started, it let up.

Morgan, James, Mom, and Dad stepped out from under the trees. They hit the trail at full stride, crunching on ice along the way.

In the cold air, the thermal areas seemed more active.

James looked at the steam drifting up from Witch Creek. "It looks like the area's on fire," he commented.

Steam eked out of vents along a hillside near the trail. Mom put her hand near one. "Yeah, it's warm," she said.

At the top of the ridge, the family paused. They looked back at Heart Lake far below and at the pink mud pot still plopping away at the top of the hill.

Dad shook his head. "There really is no place in the world like Yellowstone." He checked his watch. "It's six o'clock. We've got three hours before dark to hike five miles."

"At least the trail is mostly flat now," James recalled.

"And the storm seems to have moved on," Mom added.

"And we should be far away from that bear now," Morgan reassured herself.

The family continued hiking.

The Parkers walked as fast as they could. The trail dipped up and down, rolling over small hills.

Morgan noticed scat near the trail. "What animal left these?"

"Those are elk droppings," Mom replied.

The storm returned. Lightning flashed and illuminated the sky, followed by rolling drums of thunder.

Soon they were hiking in the rain again. The clouds made it nearly dark.

"We might need our flashlights soon," Dad called out.

Elk scat   Deer scat

It started raining harder. Hail was mixed in with the raindrops. The lightning and thunder intensified.

Mom stopped. She turned to look at Morgan and James. "Are you two okay?"

Morgan and James nodded.

"You've got to let us know if you're not," Mom urged. "The trail is soaked, it's cold, and there's lightning everywhere. This is very dangerous. I'm also worried about hypothermia, when our body temperature gets too cold. But at this point, we have no choice but to go on. We can't set up camp around here in the middle of the storm. Please let us know if you need anything or have to stop."

Morgan looked at James then at her mom. "We will," she agreed. They hiked on while rain and hail pounded down.

At the top of a small rise, Mom turned around. "Let's jog through here. It's open and exposed. I don't want to be in this spot with all the lightning around."

Like four soldiers at boot camp, the family splashed on.

The trail dipped into a forested area. Lightning ripped at the sky in front of them. Thunder boomed. Morgan and James screamed. Mom cowered and covered her head.

"What next?" Dad screamed.

They plowed on toward a grove of tall trees. In the approaching night, Mom saw movement up ahead. At first, it frightened her. Then Mom saw a flashlight going off and on. It was the Alexander family! They were gathered together again underneath their tarp.

"Come on in out of the weather!" Mark called out.

Mom led Morgan, James, and Dad toward the temporary shelter. They shuffled under and joined their neighbors from camp.

"Thanks," Dad said gratefully. "I don't know how much longer we could have gone on."

"We stopped here, thinking we'd have to set up our tent and wait out the storm," Catherine explained. "But it quickly got too cold and wet even for that, so we just jumped under the tarp."

The families sat close together. Mom, Dad, Morgan, and James formed a small circle, holding on to each other for body warmth. Their packs were propped up against a log, partially protected from the onslaught of weather.

Suddenly, a distant orange glow lit the forest. Again, the storm was letting up, only this time it revealed a sunset-filled sky. The families grabbed their backpacks and took out flashlights.

"Let's all stay in one line, no more than a stride apart," Mom directed. "And watch your footing: the trail's a mess." Mom looked again at Morgan and James, then she glanced at Dad. They all appeared capable of hiking on.

All eight hikers snaked their way into the growing darkness.

"I feel like we're in a Survivor episode," Morgan whispered to James.

"I hope no bears are around now," James whispered back.

The twilight trek continued. Lightning flashed on and off, followed by thunder. But it wasn't as close. In places, the trail was no more than a muddy stream.

Dad called out in frustration, "How much longer is this trail?"

Then, after a period of long, quiet marching, a voice behind the group shouted, "Is everyone all right up there?"

The two families stopped and turned around. A person with a flashlight was signaling them. A moment later, two backcountry rangers jogged up. "We got your note," the woman said. "And we immediately took off to make sure you got out of here safely."

"But the storm held us up," the other woman added.

"Us too," Dad said. "It was quite a storm!"

"Are all of you okay?" the woman asked.

Morgan and James nodded their heads.

"I think we are," Mom replied.

Dad told the rangers more about the grizzly.

"You did the right thing," the ranger explained. "A bear guarding a carcass is very dangerous."

"How much farther do we have to go?" James asked.

"Actually, you're almost there!" the woman responded. "We'll escort you the rest of the way."

One ranger walked to the front of the group. The other went to the back. The hikers marched on along the soaked trail, squishing and splashing around a few more bends.

James saw a light ahead. *It must be the ranger's flashlight,* he thought. But then there was another, brighter light moving from north to south.

"Stop! Look!" James shouted ecstatically. A moment later, a third light came, but this one started to slow down.

"It's cars driving on the road," Dad called out.

"Woo-hoo!" Mom shouted.

They surged forward until they arrived at the trailhead. A handful of cars were parked there. The car that slowed down had turned into the parking lot. It was a ranger patrol car.

"Welcome back to civilization!" Mom announced.

"I've never been so glad to see our car in my whole life," Dad stated.

Mom fumbled through her pockets and fished out the keys. With shaking hands, she tried to open the door. "I can't turn the keys, my hands are too cold."

Dad came over and rubbed Mom's hands. Mom put the key in the car door again and turned with her whole body.

CLICK! The door opened.

Morgan, James, Mom, and Dad dropped their packs. They took off their ponchos, left them outside, and piled into the car. Mom turned on the engine. They rolled down the windows for ventilation, and Mom turned up the heat. Dad grabbed two blankets from the back of the car and spread them across the family. Slowly the Parkers began to thaw out.

Dad stepped outside and walked to the trunk. He pulled out some dry clothes for everyone and poked his head and arms in the window. "Everyone needs to change into these right away," he instructed. Dad then turned around and loaded the packs into the back.

A moment later, the ranger patrol car drove up. A ranger got out of the car and walked up to the Parkers. "The backcountry rangers radioed in to me and told me what happened. Are all of you okay?"

"We're doing all right, especially after what we've been through," Dad replied.

"We're going to need to interview all those involved in the bear incident," the ranger said.

"I understand," Dad replied.

"But we can do that in the morning, after you get some rest," the ranger added. "I know it's been a long day."

"Are you going to close that area where the bear was?" James asked.

"Absolutely," the ranger replied. "We'll close those campsites and the trail nearby for the time being. We already called in and told the backcountry office not to issue any more permits. We can't take the chance of another encounter. By the way, where are you staying?"

"We were hoping to get a spot at the nearest campground, at Lewis Lake," Dad replied.

"I'll lead you there and help you get set up," the ranger said.

The ranger walked back to his patrol car. The backcountry rangers came over and said good-bye, then headed back out on the trail.

"It's quite a job they have," Mom commented.

"That's what I want to do when I grow up!" James announced.

Dad looked at James. "Really? After all that?"

"It seems so exciting, and you get to help people out in cool places like Yellowstone."

The Alexander family drove over and rolled down their windows. The Parkers thanked them for their help.

Dad stood outside. "I'll be right in," he told his family. Dad took off his torn shirt. He felt stinging as it rubbed against the back of his shoulder. Dad pulled his shoulder forward with his hand. He could feel several gashes and scratches across the upper part of his back. *Bear claws*, Dad realized. He put on a dry shirt and stepped into the car.

• • •

The ranger in the patrol car escorted the Parkers to the campground. Once they got out of the car, Dad told him about the scratch marks. "Can I take a look?" the ranger asked.

Dad slowly took off his shirt. The ranger examined the scratches. "You were lucky," he concluded. "These aren't too serious."

The ranger walked back to his car and pulled out a first-aid kit. "You'll need to get that cleaned up. With bears, any injury poses a high risk of infection."

The ranger began cleaning Dad's wounds. "We'll need to get pictures of the injuries in the morning," he explained. "Can I meet you back here at 9:00 a.m.?"

"Of course," Dad replied.

Once the Parkers were in dry clothes, they warmed up quickly. Dad strung up rope. They hung up all the wet clothes and gear they could find. Mom set up the tent. Finally, they threw their sleeping bags and rolled-up mattresses inside the tent. After chowing down on snack foods, the family made sure camp was clean. Morgan, James, Dad, and Mom piled inside the tent and hastily snuggled into their sleeping bags.

"That was one scary day!" Mom said. "It is wonderful that we are all safe and warm and together now."

The Parkers tried to get some sleep.

. . .

An enormous grizzly bear stood up on its hind legs and growled ferociously at Morgan. Morgan backed up several steps. She reached down to her belt and tried to grab the bear spray. The bear lunged at Morgan and swatted her hand, causing the repellent to drop to the ground. A blast of orange pepper spray shot out of the bear canister and hit a nearby tree. "Oh, no!" Morgan shouted. "All the repellent will be gone!"

"Help me!" Morgan screamed.

"HELP!"

"HELP, THERE'S A BEAR!!!"

. . .

Morgan tossed and turned in her sleeping bag.

Mom woke up. She looked at Morgan.

. . .

The grizzly continued to lumber angrily toward Morgan. She backed up and propped herself against a tree. Now Morgan had nowhere to go.

"Help!" Morgan shouted. "There's no guarantee of my safety!"

. . .

Now Dad was awake too.

Mom nudged Morgan awake. She put her arms around her. "It's okay," she said. "We're with you and it's safe. It's okay."

"You must have been having a bad dream," Dad said.

Morgan looked up at her family. "I'm glad I'm not alone on the trail with a grizzly around," she said. "I love you."

Dad smiled. "We love you too."

Lone Star in action

The early morning sun poured down on the

family's campsite. The Parkers were still inside their tent, snug in their sleeping bags. Outside, steam rose off the ground, their tent, and all the wet clothes that they'd hung up.

Campers in other sites were busy with breakfast, cleaning, or packing.

Mom heard the sounds outside. "There's a whole world going on out there."

James rolled over. "But we're nice and warm in here!"

Morgan looked at her parents. "I don't think I slept well last night."

"I think you had some nightmares, honey," Mom soothed.

"I know," Morgan recalled. "About a grizzly bear. But I don't remember a lot."

"That's probably a good thing," Dad said.

. . .

At 9:00 a.m., a car pulled into the Parkers' campsite.

Dad looked at his watch. "Right on time," he announced.

The family got dressed and met the ranger outside. He asked Dad, James, and Morgan questions about the encounter with the bear and took photographs of Dad's scratch marks.

"You did the right thing," the ranger said. "When a grizzly is that close and charging, the best thing to do is play dead and protect the back of your head and neck."

The ranger looked up from his notes. "Is there anything else you can tell me?"

James looked over. "I remember how bad the bear smelled. I don't know if it was his breath or just all over, but I think I'll remember that smell for the rest of my life."

"Well, grizzlies aren't exactly known for their hygiene," the ranger said. "But thank you for all of your help. We are going to go out there and inspect the area. It's the only way to keep the public, and that bear, safe."

The ranger drove away.

Dad took a deep breath. "This whole bear thing wasn't exactly the experience I had planned for in Yellowstone!"

"Neither is having to hurry out of camp in the morning," Mom said. "But campground checkout is in a few minutes."

"I've got an idea," Dad said. "Let's just throw everything in the car and head over to the Old Faithful Lodge for breakfast."

Mom looked at Dad. "Now that sounds like a plan!"

• • •

The lodge was busy with tourists. The Parkers waited in line to get into the restaurant. Once they were seated, the family walked over to the breakfast buffet.

James spooned a huge serving of potatoes and two cinnamon rolls onto his plate. Morgan doused three pieces of French toast with maple syrup and powdered sugar. Mom sprinkled granola and fruit over her extra-large bowl of yogurt. Dad took a gigantic blueberry muffin and a double-sized portion of scrambled eggs and toast.

Eventually, they all met back at their table with food piled high on their plates.

"I guess I was really hungry," James said sheepishly.

"Me too," Morgan added.

"Us too," Mom said. "Did we eat much at all yesterday?"

They all started chowing down.

"What else are we going to do today?" James asked. "We now have a whole extra day in the park."

"You're right," Mom answered. "I hadn't thought about that."

Dad rubbed his hand on his scruffy beard and looked off into the distance. "Let's do something a bit more tame today, okay? James and Morgan, can you figure that out for us?"

"Okay," Morgan agreed.

After breakfast, they wandered around the lodge and bought souvenirs. James got a poster of a grizzly. "I don't know if I want to put this up in my bedroom or not," he told his family.

Morgan bought a poster of Old Faithful. Dad bought a book about bears, and Mom bought one on wolves.

Dad noticed the couches that people were lounging on. "I could just sit in one of those and sleep all day," he said.

Morgan elbowed her brother. "What about Lone Star?"

"Lone Star?" Dad asked.

"Yeah, that's Morgan's and my idea for today," James stated. "We looked at the park map and realized that the Lone Star Geyser Trail is on our way out of the park."

"And it's a short, easy hike," Morgan said.

"And it's a popular trail. There should be a lot of people on it," James added.

"I'm convinced," Dad said. "We all keep talking about seeing another geyser; here's our chance."

The family drove to the Lone Star Geyser trailhead. Mom got out her bear spray. Dad grabbed what was left of his.

They began walking on the flat, wide trail following a babbling brook. James and Morgan stayed close to their parents. They watched the forest for any sign of a bear.

Several other hikers were also on the trail. A few people on mountain bikes zipped by.

"It's nice to see so many people around," Mom said.

Soon they approached an open area.

In the middle of a barren meadow was a large, solitary cone. Steam spewed out of the top of it. Hot water sloshed over its sides.

"Now I can see where Lone Star got its name," Mom said. "There's nothing else nearby."

The family looked around. The hill behind the geyser was devoid of plants. There were steam vents and small areas of boiling water percolating out of the ground. And, there was a large group of people gathered at Lone Star, waiting.

James saw several people sitting off to the side, writing in notebooks. "Hey! It's Tom!"

Morgan, James, Mom, and Dad walked over.

"Hi!" Morgan greeted Tom.

Tom looked up. "Hi again, my old friends."

"It's a small world, isn't it?" Dad commented.

"Yes, it's quite a coincidence that we keep running into each other," Tom agreed. "Because it is such a large park."

"Are you writing down things about the geyser?" James asked.

"Exactly," Tom answered. Then he thought for a moment. "Would you all like to join us and become geyser gazers?"

"Okay," James said. "What do we have to do?"

"It's the easiest club in the world to be a part of," Tom explained. "We write down the behavior of geysers and keep track of dates and times. We post information in a logbook at the visitor center at Old Faithful. And we post some of our notes on our club website. That way, all of us can keep in touch with the geysers year-round, even if we aren't in Yellowstone."

"I've got paper from my journal in my pack," Morgan said.

The Parkers sat down and joined the other geyser gazers. Morgan, James, Mom, and Dad began writing notes.

Mom wrote, "The cone must be over ten feet high. And, it's all by itself. Steam and water are coming out of the top. It seems like it's going to erupt, but it hasn't so far. . . ."

Dad wrote, "This whole area is cooking. There are little steaming spots all over the place. Of course, this is Yellowstone. Nothing that we see surprises me anymore."

James wrote, "Tom just told me that Lone Star erupts every three hours or so. And we are here, just over three hours after its last eruption. I guess that's why there are so many people out here. . . . I think this might be our lucky day!"

Morgan pulled out the park map she and James were keeping track of animal sightings on. First she put a big X by Heart Lake and wrote: "Grizzly encounter, here!!!" Then she wrote about Lone Star. "It seems like the geyser is calming down. But I can hear it gurgling, and I hear a humming sound."

Suddenly, steam started to spew out of the cone more intensely.

Then, quickly, a large spray of water blasted into the air.

The geyser gazers stood up.

"It's so strong—like there's a fire hydrant in there," Morgan said.

Water continued to shoot out of Lone Star's cone and head straight into the air. Steam and mist whipped away from the powerful spray and drifted onto the geyser gazers. They moved away from the warm, natural shower and continued watching the geyser's performance.

And it kept on going.

"It doesn't seem real," James stated. "It's been going on for so long!"

"And we're so close to it," Morgan added.

"It's kind of like being at a fireworks show," Dad concluded.

Lone Star kept pumping out water. Eventually, the eruption phased into mostly steam pouring out of the cone.

"Now it looks more like smoke from a train," Morgan said.

Tom looked over at the Parkers, grinning. "Now, that is an eruption!"

James leaned toward Tom. "Is this your favorite geyser?"

Tom smiled. "It is right now!"

James pulled out his journal.

This is James Parker reporting.

I'm sitting here at Lone Star Geyser. It has been erupting for almost thirty minutes, although it seems like it's almost over. I wish we were hiking to Shoshone Geyser Basin. Or sitting by the Boiling River. Or seeing other geysers erupt, like Steamboat and Echinus. I want to see more! Yellowstone is such an unusual place. As Dad said, "There's nothing in the world like it!" So what are my ten favorite sights? Here goes:

1. Lone Star Geyser
2. The Grand Canyon of the Yellowstone
3. Mystic Falls
4. Old Faithful
5. Storm Point
6. Grand Prismatic Spring
7. Dragon's Mouth
8. Artist Paint Pots
9. Mammoth Hot Springs
10. Grebe Lake

Anyway, I am officially stating in this journal that I will be reading up on Yellowstone's geysers on the geyser gazer Web site, and I will be back!

Reporting from Yellowstone,

James Parker

And Morgan wrote:

Dear Diary,

It's the last day and the last few minutes of our trip in Yellowstone. I can't believe how sad I feel. Can't we stay a week longer? Or more?

It's going to be a lot of work going through all my pictures and labeling the places we've visited. Will I remember the names of all the pools, geysers, steam vents, and hot springs? Maybe our book on Yellowstone's geysers will help me identify them.

At least we have that map where we kept track of the animals we saw. Boy, I will never forget what happened to us at Heart Lake!

I see that James wrote a Top Ten list of sights in Yellowstone. I agree with it, but I would also add: Uncle Tom's Trail, Norris Geyser Basin, Fairy Falls, Firehole Drive.

But **my** Top Ten list is for animal sightings. The best ones were:

1. The black bear near Tower Falls
2. The coyote eating the marmot at Storm Point
3. The elk on the lawn at Mammoth Hot Springs
4. Hearing wolves at night
5. The bison on the road and chasing someone in Hayden Valley
6. The bald eagle at Grebe Lake
7. The moose at Grebe Lake
8. The elk in the meadows near Madison
9. The grizzly bear at Heart Lake
10. The bighorn sheep on Mt. Sheridan (Mom wanted me to include that)

I somberly sign off from Yellowstone,
Morgan

The family gathered up their belongings. Morgan jotted down Tom's geyser gazer website. They said good-bye to Tom and the other geyser gazers. Slowly and silently, they hiked back to their car. They piled in and drove east, then turned south at Grant Junction.

As they approached the Heart Lake trailhead, Dad slowed the car down and turned into the parking lot.

"What are you doing?" Morgan asked.

"You'll see," Dad responded.

Dad drove over to the trailhead. "Yep, that's what I thought! They already put up a sign."

The sign read:

WARNING: BEAR FREQUENTING AREA. THERE IS NO GUARANTEE OF YOUR SAFETY ON THIS TRAIL! TRAIL CLOSED UNTIL FURTHER NOTICE BEYOND MT. SHERIDAN JUNCTION DUE TO GRIZZLY BEAR ACTIVITY AND A CARCASS IN THE AREA.

"Well it's certainly important to warn people," Mom commented.

Morgan rolled down her window and snapped a picture of the sign. "Just reading it gives me the chills."

"Me too," Dad said. He moved his shoulder, but didn't feel any pain.

• • •

Soon they left Yellowstone behind and quickly entered another national park. Massive, sharp-edged, stark mountains punctured the sky to the right of the road. The peaks were capped with snowfields and small glaciers.

Dad stared out the window in awe. "The Grand Tetons!" he exclaimed.

"Next time," Mom stated. "Next time."